Spring Break
Murder
Linnea West

Spring Break Murder

•Chapter One•

The clouds outside the airplane window had been white and fluffy when we took off in Minnesota but the closer we got to Florida, the more gray and ominous they were. I didn't think that was a very good sign, but then again I hadn't been the one to think taking a spring break trip to Florida was a good idea.

I think part of my hangup was the term "spring break trip" which brings up visions of crowded beaches, sunburns, and too much to drink. At the ripe old age of 30, none of that sounded appealing. I would have much preferred to spend this week on some sort of staycation in the downright frigid climate of Minnesota. There were plenty of hotels with indoor waterparks within driving distance of my hometown of Shady Lake, where we could just pretend we were in a tropical climate while we lounged poolside.

That would have been the case if it wasn't for my best friend, Mandy, who was currently snoring in the seat next to me with a purple sleep mask over her eyes. She had volunteered to take the middle seat as she was planning to sleep the flight away. I'm not sure how she could possibly be comfortable, but somehow Mandy had fallen asleep sitting straight up with one of those pillows around her neck. I was amazed at her ability to not slump over to one side or the other.

Mandy had planned this entire trip for us because her parents had retired to Florida. When Mandy and I had graduated high school, Mandy's parents had hightailed it out of our small Minnesota town, retiring to an RV that they parked permanently in Florida. Mandy had taken over running the Donut Hut which, hands down, made the best donuts in Shady Lake.

But this week the Donut Hut would be shut down. Originally, Mandy was supposed to take this trip with her long-time boyfriend Trevor, but he hadn't been able to get time off of work. When Mandy told me that, I had to scoff a little bit because the only reason he hadn't been able to get the time off was because he had waited too long to put in the request. He worked as an emergency dispatcher and it was first come, first serve when it came to time off. The emergency lines still needed to run even if it was vacation time.

Trevor and I were still not super fond of each other, but I had come around and we had a sort of unspoken agreement to get along because Mandy loved us both and we didn't want her to have to choose one of us over the other. So I kept my not-so-nice remarks about his immaturity to myself and he

4

mostly just steered clear of me.

I pulled out our itinerary for the week. When Mandy's mom Sally heard that I was coming along, she had immediately jumped into action, wanting to show me around everywhere. Ever since we were little, Mandy and I had been so close that we were practically sisters. Sally and Bill considered me like their second child and this would be the first time I'd seen them in person since they retired after I had moved away to college.

"This is your captain speaking," came a tinny voice over the intercom. "It looks like we will be experiencing a little bit of turbulence but don't worry, it is just a little rain storm."

True to the pilot's word, the plane started to shake around slightly as raindrops ran down the window. I didn't enjoy flying on a good day and I really didn't like flying on a stormy day. My stomach lurched as the plane dipped a bit and I grabbed the armrests to hold on tight.

"Yowch," shrieked Mandy waking up with a start as my nails dug into her hand, which I had forgotten was occupying my armrest.

She ripped off her sleep mask and rubbed the back of her hand. I tried to look apologetic, but that was interrupted by another dip of the plane that sent me clutching the armrest again. Mandy seemed to take pity on me and my absolute terror.

I am obviously not much of a traveler. I would much rather take a road trip or even a trip on a train than in an airplane. I wouldn't say I'm scared of flying, but something about the idea that a metal container weighing a few tons being able to carry me safely through the air to my destination just didn't sit right with me.

"It's going to be okay, Tessa," Mandy said. She patted my now white, clawlike hand that was grasping onto the armrest for dear life. "It's just a bit of turbulence."

I tried to give her a little smile, but judging from the small smile that flashed across her face before it was hidden away, I had only managed to grimace in her direction. Reaching into my bag, I grabbed out a package of snack mix and tried to focus on eating all of it in order. I preferred to eat the breadsticks first, then the little rye chips, followed by the pretzels and then finally the cereal pieces, which were my favorite.

As I snacked my way through the much too salty snack, the face of my boyfriend floated up to the forefront of my thoughts. Officer Max Marcus always laughed at how I eat my snacks in a particular way. By now, he knew the exact order I liked to eat any sort of snack that came with multiple shapes or flavors and he teased me about it every time.

Max and I were once high school sweethearts.

But after graduation, I had gone off to college while he stayed behind in town and we had grown apart. We ended up married to different people but through a cruel twist of fate, we were both widowed within months of each other. My husband Peter died in a car accident on the way to work one morning while Max's wife Anne had passed away from cancer.

After spiraling down into darkness after my Peter died, my parents recognized that I needed help and they had rescued me, packing up my apartment and moving everything back to Shady Lake for me. It was a bit strange living with my parents again, but it was even stranger now because after most of my siblings and I had moved out, they had renovated their old Victorian style house and made it into a bed and breakfast with a new wing added on where they lived. When I moved in, I actually took over what was supposed to be their personal library but now that I was really getting my feet back under me, I hoped to be moving out soon.

When Max and I got back together, we originally wanted to keep things very casual. We were both still grieving and didn't want to jump into a serious fling before we had actually sorted out our emotions. I had even been casually dating another man, Clark Hutchins, but things had cooled down with him just as Max and I decided we wanted to take the next step in our relationship.

I closed my eyes, trying to focus on Max's handsome face instead of my stomach, which was still turning somersaults. Max was short and stocky, but in a muscular way. He worked as a police officer for the town of Shady Lake, so he made sure to stay physically fit. His sandy blond hair and blue eyes were still exactly the same as the boy I had started dating so long ago. Max was the kind of person who never really seemed to age. Sure, he seemed a bit more mature but if he was compared to his pictures from high school, he looked exactly the same.

On the other hand, I suppose I still looked mostly the same also. The only thing that had really changed was my waistline, thanks to my proclivity for baked goods specifically the ones from the Donut Hut. Mandy didn't approve of my sweets-eating habit but couldn't help herself from bringing me a fresh donut every once in a while. Heck, even this morning she had been ready and waiting with a day-old sugar twist donut for me as the shuttle van to the airport pulled up to her apartment.

I must have nodded off thinking of Max's ruggedly handsome face because the next thing I knew, I woke up to another tinny announcement from the pilot. I rubbed my eyes a little, trying to bring everything back into focus.

"We are starting our descent," he said. "The air temperature is 75 degrees, which should feel extra good for all of you Minnesotans today."

A small cheer erupted from the plane along with a bigger cheer when the plane landed and we could see palm trees out the window as we taxied to the gate. Mandy, the seasoned traveler she pretended she was, simply put her hand on my arm as I rushed to try to gather my things and get off of the plane.

"Just wait," she said. "No sense in being stuck trying to get out. Relax a little more and we will get off eventually."

I plopped back into my seat and grabbed the trashy magazine I hadn't had time to read yet and paged through while we waited for the plane to empty. Once most of the passengers had gone by we gathered our things and casually exited. Mandy was right; that was much better than trying to be the first ones off the plane.

Even better was the fact that the plane's luggage had already been unloaded by the time we got to the baggage claim. Instead of pacing around, we got to just saunter up and grab our bags off of the half empty carousel. I had followed Mandy's advice and put a big, multi-colored pom-pom ball on my black suitcase so I could spot it right away and spot it right away I did.

"Mandy! Tessa!"

We whirled around to see Sally running in the automatic doors. Her arms were up over her head as she squealed, looking like a young girl. She was in her early 60's, but if I didn't know her age I would have pegged her at least ten years younger than that.

"I'm so happy to see you girls," Sally squealed as she crashed into us, a bundle of joy and sweet perfume wrapped up in a sleeveless polo shirt and knee length shorts. She wore a beautiful pair of pearl earrings and pinned to the front of her shirt was a big pin that had a picture of some tasteful flapper girls and it said "THE DOLLS" over it. At the bottom, it had Sally's name etched on it. I wondered what it meant, but I didn't have time to ask as Sally hustled us out the door.

"Let's go, your father is parked in a no parking zone," she said, scurrying out into the bright sunshine in front of us.

Mandy and I grabbed our suitcases and followed behind. Sure enough, a big maroon truck was parked just outside the door in a spot clearly marked LOADING ZONE. Mandy's father Bill was calmly ignoring a man who was yelling at him to move the truck and waved at us as we walked out.

"See, my girls are right there," Bill said, flashing a smile towards the grumpy parking man.

He strode toward us and grabbed our suitcases, tossing them into the bed of the truck as Sally opened the door to the backseat. Mandy climbed in first, crawling over to the far side as I hauled myself up into the backseat next to her.

I dug through my purse, pushing aside the trashy magazine and my miniature flashlight to find my sunglasses. As we drove down the highway, I watched the palm trees go by, happy to be taking a break from snowy Minnesota. The only thing that could make this vacation better was if Max was here with me.

•Chapter Two•

The first thing that greeted us at the RV park was a gigantic, barn-like building painted in red and white stripes. A big sign stretched over the entrance to the park that said WELCOME TO CANDY CANE PARK. The big, patterned building was labeled CANDY CANE PALACE in gigantic letters and for just a moment, I wondered if the entire park was Christmas themed.

But it must be just a name because the rest of the park looked like what I thought an RV park should look like. Rows and rows of mobile homes were as far as the eye could see with palm trees dotted up and down the streets. The Christmas theme did extend to the street names, I noticed, as we drove past Pine Tree Place and North Pole Avenue.

As we crept slowly through the park, Sally practically hung out the window chatting at everyone we drove by. She was just like Mandy; not only did she know everyone, but she was friends with everyone. Apparently she was just as good at gossiping as Mandy because everyone we passed asked if 'the girls' were here yet. At that point, Sally rolled down the back windows and we were made to wave and smile at everyone we passed until I felt like I was part of a float in the Fourth of July parade.

We pulled onto Santa Claus Street and the truck turned into the second driveway on the right. A large RV sat with a more permanent sun room and covered deck attached to the side of it. A large banner attached to the sunroom and a palm tree hung over the deck reading "Welcome Mandy and Tessa" and a small group of older women were standing on the deck, waving, hooting and hollering at us as Bill stopped the truck.

"Oh the Welcome Committee," Sally cheered as she ripped off her seatbelt and threw herself out of the truck before Bill could even manage to shift it into park. She dashed up the stairs and into the arms of the women. After a big group hug, she turned and joined the women, who were starting to chant as Mandy and I stepped out of the truck.

"Welcome to our glorious park. We hope you'll stay a spell. If you decide to overstay your vacation, we promise we won't tell!"

At that end of the chant, the women came down the stairs, surrounding Mandy and I in a sea of gray hair and the smell of sunscreen and perfume. I was hugging friendly lady after friendly lady who all seemed to know my name. I squeezed them back with a smile plastered on my face. If I hadn't been raised in a small town, this would seem strange. But Shady Lake had prepared me for meeting strangers who inexplicably knew me.

13

"Okay Dolls," Bill said as he walked up rolling both of our suitcases behind him. "Let the girls breathe a little. Also, show me to the cake."

The ladies all laughed and as a big blob of people, we moved up the steps and onto the giant deck which was obviously used for entertaining. The deck was smattered with tables and chairs with a large table set up under a window against the wall of the sun room. A large sheet cake sat in the middle with a large picture of Mandy and I as teenagers frosted onto it surrounded by other snack trays of food.

Each woman quickly introduced herself. Besides Sally, there were Kathy and Karen, who were twins who appeared to be identical and were even dressed in coordinating outfits. Susie wore a necklace with a bicycle charm and was so fit she looked like a yoga instructor. Louise seemed to be a bit on the outskirts of the crew, so I couldn't tell much about her. There was also Marie, who was wearing a large gaudy necklace and had so many bangles on her arm that she clinked anytime she moved, and Lynn, whose hair was put up in an almost impossibly high, but still chic up-do. I tried my hardest to remember each woman's name, but I knew I would forget most of them. I remember faces but names go in one ear and out the other. I did notice, however, that each one was wearing a pin that matched the one Sally had clipped to her shirt and each one was personalized, which would definitely help me not make a fool of myself when I inevitably forgot their names.

After we all got a piece of cake and settled into the shade of the deck, the ladies finally stopped talking a mile a minute. I ended up sitting at a table with Louise Templeton. Louise was a short woman with a gray bob haircut. She was wearing a khaki skort with a lime green button up top that was just a few shades too bright to be elegant. A large, gold necklace was hanging around her neck, so large and shiny that it couldn't possibly be real gold. At least, I assume it wasn't since Louise lived in an RV.

"I'm just so glad you are here," Louise said, patting my hand. "Sally has been talking about you and Tessa coming for a while. Of course I've met Mandy before, but you are like her second daughter! Getting you down here was a long time coming."

"I was glad to leave behind the snowy tundra to hang out here for a little while," I said, looking around at the palm trees.

"Well I come from Minnesota originally and my son still lives there," she said with a twinkle in her eye. "By the way, are you seeing anyone? My son is about your age and I'm always on the lookout for a lovely young lady like yourself to set him up with."

"Sorry, I have a boyfriend," I said, my thoughts flashing once again to Max. "But I bet your son loves that you do that."

Louise threw her head back and let out a large, endearing guffaw. I was glad she had picked up on my humor rather than getting upset. I knew that if she was good friends with Sally, she had to have a good sense of humor. I took the break from Louise doing the talking to ask her about something that had caught my eye. There was a large sign above the table that said "Clubhouse of the Guys and Dolls."

"What does that sign mean?" I asked, pointing to it before I took another bite of cake.

"Oh that's the name of our club," Louise said as she tapped me on the arm. Her eyes were shining and she looked like an excited teenager as the words came spilling out of her mouth. "It is our social club. I mean it's mostly the Dolls, but sometimes we make our husbands come to meetings and they are obviously the Guys. We meet here once a week and take it upon ourselves to organize the social get-togethers here at the park. We welcome visitors, find new activities and volunteer opportunities to offer, and sometimes we just drink mimosas and play cards. It really depends on the day."

"That sounds just like the Sally I know," I said, thinking back to all of the clubs and activities Sally had been involved in when she lived in Shady Lake. While Mandy wasn't quite as busy, she was just as involved in the community as her mother. "So can just anyone join your club?"

"Oh no, of course not," Louise said with a smile. "I mean we invite people, but we want to maintain a certain level of participation in our club. Before we made these rules, anyone could join and believe me, it was a lot of people sayin' they were in the club and not doing anything to help. Sally changed all of that when she moved down here."

"So what rules did you put in place?" I asked. This was starting to sound more like a high school clique than a social club for senior citizens. The membership pins were about the only thing that set them apart.

"Oh, well people who want to join have to put in an application," Louise said. "Once a year we solicit applications and then we host a cocktail hour here at the clubhouse where we can vet the candidates."

I looked around at the group. There were only seven women here. How many people could they possibly let in every year? For some reason, this club intrigued me.

"How many people are allowed in each year?" I asked.

"It depends," Louise said as she had another bite of cake. "Some years, no one is allowed in. Most years we allow one new member. But we want this club to stay exclusive, so we can't just let everyone in."

She laughed a sort of choked laugh that made it seem like she knew just how unfair this selection process was. Louise stabbed the last bit of cake on her plate and started waving it around as she gestured.

"I'll let you in on a little secret," she said conspiratorially. I couldn't help but watch the cake, afraid the delicious bite would fall right off her fork. "I was the last member allowed in and I'm not even sure why in the world they selected me. I used to be a dowdy old fuddy-duddy. But they apparently saw some potential in me and took pity on me. I like to think it's because I'm pure of heart."

She gave another odd laugh before eating the bite of cake off her fork with a little raise of her eyebrows letting me know she trusted me with her secret.

"Honestly though, I have no clue why they chose me," she said, still talking just above a whisper. I could tell by the way she said it that she wasn't actually looking for any input from me, so I put another big bite of cake in my mouth as I leaned forward to hear her better. "And we haven't let in a new member since, so I have no idea what the criteria actually is. But I know there are several people around here who are not happy about the way business is run by the Dolls."

My mouth was full of cake, but I managed to bulge my eyes enough to let her know I was

18

surprised. Louise smirked, obviously pleased at how I was receiving the gossip. As the lowest ranking member of the Dolls, I'm sure she never got the pleasure of sharing the juiciest news.

"Word around the park is that the Poodle Woman herself Cindy Parker and her little underling Hilda Brown have tried to join the Dolls unsuccessfully for years," Louise said. I nodded along, pretending to know who she was talking about. A glance around the deck let me know that no one else was paying attention to us, caught up in their own loud conversations and snack eating.

"Tell me more," I said. This was almost as good as the trashy magazines I like to read every once in a while and unlike Mandy, I'm okay listening to a little gossip every once in a while.

"At first, Cindy was okay with not getting in because like I said, they don't really let people in," Louise said. "But when they let me in a few years ago, she was not happy. She actually ripped down the congratulations poster the other Dolls put up for me. After that, Cindy's been on a bit of a manhunt to try and get us kicked out of the park. Thankfully the man who runs the park doesn't care to kick us out because we are good tenants. Cindy is the pain in the patoot."

Before I could say anything else, Bill stood up and waited for the chatting to die down a bit. Sally and Mandy were the last ones still chatting, both of them eager to wrap up their conversation rather than have to interrupt it. Bill looked on, tapping his foot for comedic effect. Finally, the two ladies stopped talking and turned to face Bill.

"I'm so sorry to interrupt your conversation," Bill said, a note of sarcasm in his voice and a large smile on his face. "But it is time for Sally and I to take the girls to lunch. Don't worry, we will all be out to bob later before I shut the pool down tonight. See you all there!"

Bobbing? I shot a glance towards Mandy, but she was back to chatting her mother's ear off. Maybe it was just another word for swimming, since Bill mentioned the pool. I guess I'd find out later.

"I'll see you later dear," Louise said, her gray hair shaking around her face as she patted my hand. "And just keep that little bit about Cindy to yourself."

I nodded back at her and assured her I would tell no one about the anger of the Poodle Woman and her underling. As Louise shuffled away with the rest of the ladies, I wondered if that included not telling Mandy. As I pushed myself up out of my chair, I decided I'd wait. I wanted to at least see this Poodle Woman before I shared the juicy news.

•Chapter Three•

After a very exciting lunch at a popular food buffet where I stuffed myself with delicious pizza while Mandy's plate was mounded with the biggest salad I've ever seen, we headed back to the park to go bobbing, whatever that was.

"Change into your swimsuits girls and I'll get your noodles," Sally said when she reemerged from her bedroom. Sally practically floated out the door, leaving us to dig through our suitcases for our bathing suits.

"Do you know what in the world bobbing is?" I asked once the door slammed shut.

"Yes, I do," Mandy said, her eyes twinkling. She was enjoying this a bit too much "But I'm not going to tell you."

I started to protest, but Mandy simply dashed through the door to the RV's bedroom, calling over her shoulder to me as she shut the door to change.

"Don't worry, it's fun," she said.

I harumphed to myself, but decided that I was on vacation and should see this as a happy surprise. I sat on the little couch and waited for Mandy to come out. The RV was a comfortable place with a sofa that folded out to the bed Mandy and I would be sleeping on. There were also two tan recliners, each one claimed by one of Mandy's parents. The kitchen was a little galley style with appliances that seemed to be three-quarter sized. I'd never spent any considerable amount of time in an RV, so this inside look was intriguing to me.

I peeked out the window again and looked at the sun room that had been added on. The idea of adding a permanent room onto a mobile home seemed a little silly at first, but most of the RVs down here had some sort of permanent structure added and it doubled the living space. Instead of having a dining table in the RV, there was a larger one out in the sunroom that could accommodate lots of guests. Against one wall was a bar with a full-sized refrigerator behind it. I had the feeling that the clubhouse for the Dolls extended into the sunroom. I was starting to think it would be pretty cool to have a clubhouse like this, but seeing as I was the girl living in her parent's library, I didn't have much say in any additional construction projects.

"Your turn," Mandy said as she slammed the sliding door open. She came out in a dark heather green, high-waisted bikini. Somehow she managed to look amazing without looking like she was trying to dress like a teenager. I envied her natural sense of style.

I grabbed my swimsuit and switched places with Mandy. After shutting the door, I turned around and looked at this half of the RV. Through the door was the bedroom and a small bathroom. Most of the bedroom was taken up by a large, queen size bed that was covered with throw pillows and a floral duvet. I assumed that the small cabinet on each side of the head of the bed held Bill and Sally's clothes.

There were two more doors, one on each side of me, in what seemed to be the world's tiniest hallway. I opened the one on the left and a bunch of hanging clothes popped out. Okay, so it was a closet. I slowly closed the door as I shoved the clothes back in so I didn't shut anything in the door.

The door on the other side was the world's smallest toilet room. I wondered if I was supposed to actually shut the door when I used it because it was so tiny. The sound of a bird chirp made me look up. The tiny room came with a tiny, covered skylight. I guess that's a nice addition.

What caught my attention the most about this half of the RV was the shower. It was kind of an open-plan type shower. It was a shower stall, but it was just placed in the corner of the bedroom. There was a curtain you could draw around it if you wanted to. I guess when I need to shower, I'll have to tell everyone not to come back here. On the other hand, at least the shower wasn't in a tiny room like the toilet was. I knew I'd have enough claustrophobia just using the bathroom.

"Are you dressed yet?" Mandy said, rapping impatiently on the plywood door.

"Almost, just hold on," I yelled back. I hadn't even started getting changed yet.

I quickly pulled off my clothes and pulled on the black, one-piece swimsuit that Mandy convinced me I should buy. I took a peek in the mirror hanging on the back of the toilet door and I had to admit that I looked good. Mandy was annoyingly dead-on with her fashion sense for both herself and for me. I made a mental note to listen to her more often when it comes to clothes.

Mandy and I emerged from the sunroom onto the deck and were greeted by Sally and Bill, each holding two pool noodles. Each one was a different color with one of our names written on it. Mandy was handed the yellow noodle and mine was red. I looked from them to Mandy, still trying to figure out what in the world we were doing.

"I'm just going to come out and ask," I said. "What in the world is bobbing?"

"Oh dear, I suppose we didn't actually explain," Sally said. "Well all of us old people can't really swim, so what we do is bob. Everyone has a pool noodle and they use them to bob around the pool."

"And as keeper of the pool, let me tell you the rule," Bob said. He puffed up his chest, obviously enjoying the prestige of being the leader. "Everyone must label their noodle with their name because we used to have problems with people leaving them behind. Every night when I close up the pool, I collect any pool noodles that have been left behind. If someone leaves their noodle behind three times, we fine them."

"What else do you have to do as the keeper of the pool?" I asked.

"Every night I have to make sure the pool is cleared out. We don't want anyone in there late at night when there won't be help available if they need it."

"And how did you become the leader?" I asked.

"I was appointed keeper of the pool by the Guys and Dolls," Bill said with a large smile on his face. "Now the Keeper says we should get a move on."

We walked together down Santa Claus Street towards the massive Candy Cane Palace. A large concrete patio extended from the back of the building. One section was surrounded by a fence and bushes, hiding whatever was on the other side. I had to assume it must be the pool but judging by the size, the pool was probably more of an exaggerated hole in the ground filled with water.

"There's the pool, girls," Bill said as he gestured towards the bushes, putting my curiosity at rest.

Hidden between two bushes was a little gate that Bill unlatched and held open for us. Just as I suspected, the kidney shaped pool was not nearly as big as I assumed it would be. It was, however, just the right size for about twenty people at a time to float around on their pool noodles.

"Hey-yo!" came the cheers from the pool. All of the Dolls were already there waiting for us. Each one had a husband with them and they all seemed to be matched sets. Susie's husband appeared to still lift weights everyday as he was impossibly buff for an older man. Marie's husband had at least four gold chain necklaces around his neck while she still wore her bangles and other jewelry in the pool. She wasn't the only one who kept her jewelry on because I spotted Susie's bicycle necklace also. Lynn's husband had a very full head of hair that was gelled up into a sky-high pompadour that almost rivaled Lynn's up-do. Louise's husband looked just a bit out of place, just like his wife usually did. His hair was styled in a well-done combover, which is to say he had enough hair to kind of pull it off, but it was still obvious that he was hiding a bald spot. And Kathy and Karen's husbands looked so much alike that I wondered if they were actually twins also. I made a mental note to ask Sally later, just for curiosity's sake.

We found some empty pool chairs where we set our towels and stripped off the shorts we'd

26

thrown over our swimsuits. Even though the pool was a bit small, there were plenty of chairs and I decided that I would come down here tomorrow with a book if I could find a small chunk of time in the busy schedule that Sally had put together for us.

One end of the pool had a wide staircase leading down into the shallow end of the water. I assumed by the fact that everyone's hair was dry that jumping into the pool was a no-no. So Mandy and I grabbed our noodles and followed Bill and Sally down the stairs. The water was warm, almost like a bathtub. I chuckled to myself, thinking about how they probably heated the pool for those "cold" days which would be like a breath of summer back in Minnesota. Well no matter what, it felt good today.

I watched Sally and mimicked how she used her noodle. She held each end in one hand and pushed the middle down, sitting in the middle almost like she was on a playground swing. That seemed to be a much more mature way of bobbing, considering I had been thinking I'd straddle it like I was riding a hobby horse.

"Isn't this the life, girls?" Bill asked as he floated by us. "Soak it up because after a week we're putting you back on a plane to the North Pole!"

We all chuckled and Mandy splashed a little water at her father who put up his hands to block the attack. We all laughed even harder as Bill lost his balance and tipped over backward, dunking himself into the water. I was laughing so hard my stomach hurt as Bill emerged from the depths of the pool with a giant smile on his face. Looking around, everyone was laughing so hard that I wondered if anyone else would dunk themselves.

"Splashing is against the pool rules," came an acidic voice from the direction of the pool gate. "You'd think the daughter of the pool keeper would know that. I hope this isn't a case of special privileges for the golden child."

The joyful atmosphere of the pool immediately sunk to the bottom as the laughter and smiles melted into looks of contempt. I turned around to see who this lovely sounding character was.

Standing just inside the fence was a bitter looking old woman wearing a house dress with a large, loud floral pattern that contrasted with the expression on her face. Her silver hair was curled so tightly that it sat high above her head and then cascaded around her face and down to her shoulders in waves that were just a bit too tight to be fashionable.

Behind her stood a woman who was so hunched over that she looked like she was almost going to get down and do a somersault. For a moment I felt bad, thinking she may have a hunchback. But another look told me she was just so deferential to the woman in front of her that she practically bowed to her constantly so as not to stand up taller than her.

It didn't take a genius to figure out that we had just been introduced to Cindy Parker, the Poodle Woman and her lackey, Hilda Brown.

•Chapter Four•

"Hello there Cindy, Hilda," Bill said, ever the cheerful welcomer. "Come on into the pool with us. What can I do ya for today?"

Bill's happy greeting only seemed to make Cindy more upset. I wasn't sure how Hilda felt because her face was turned down towards the ground and the top of her head didn't betray her feelings one way or the other.

"First off, you know we don't go in the pool," Cindy said.

"We know, Cindy," Louise said. "You wouldn't want to ruin that hair of yours."

Cindy put one hand up to pat her hair, not seeming to understand the jab that went along with it. Hilda did, though because her head snapped up and her dark, beady eyes searched the pool, trying to figure out who had said it. I couldn't help but think that the task of picking out Cindy's attacker would be much easier if she had been looking up to actually see who had said the offending remark.

"Of course I don't want to ruin this hair," Cindy said. "I spend hours on this hair each week. I'm not going to ruin it simply so I can float around this giant bathtub in everyone's germs. Besides, it probably isn't even clean."

"Cindy, if you have a problem with the pool, you can take it up with me privately," Bill said. "I'm the keeper of the pool and I take my job quite seriously."

"You only take it seriously because you like the power that comes with it," Cindy snapped. Hilda was standing behind her, vigorously nodding her head up and down. "I wouldn't tell you the problems if you paid me. I go right to the top. I take all of my complaints straight to Tom Parks."

"We know," came a chorus of voices from the pool. I looked around. Who in the world was Tom Parks?

"Tom Parks owns the park," Sally said, sensing my confusion. "And yes, he realizes the correlation between his job and his last name."

I nodded. We hadn't even been here for an entire day yet and already we were embroiled in the drama of the RV park. I was actually a little surprised that a retirement community could have so much drama. It was almost better than a reality TV show.

"Well if you want to get anything done in this park, you have to go to the top," Cindy said, charging on in her speech. "It isn't like you lot do anything besides sit at that stupid clubhouse and eat and drink while you decide how to make everyone else feel unwelcome. And that wouldn't be so bad if you didn't constantly break the rules of the park."

"Cindy, we don't really break the rules of the park," Bill said. "Besides, most of them are more like guidelines than anything else and the others are rules that are utterly pointless. Why should we have to limit the number of chairs on our deck? Does it matter if we have more than the allowed four chairs? We have a large deck and lots of friends. Are we supposed to only allow two of them to sit with us because of that rule?"

The group in the pool quietly tittered with laughter while Cindy's snarl deepened. Her gnarled fists curled up into balls against her gaudy house dress. In that moment, I almost felt bad for her. Obviously this was a woman who had some sort of deep hurt somewhere and everyone laughing at her did not help.

"It isn't about the chairs, Bill," Cindy bellowed, surprising me with her volume. The voice that came out was so mismatched from her that the laughter in the pool immediately stopped.

"It's about making sure that people follow the rules," she continued. "Rules are important and are made to be followed. I know you all think you are special and you can break the rules because of your stupid little club, but they apply to you also. Mr. High and Mighty keeper of the pool has to follow them just like all of us other lowly park-dwellers."

"Excuse me, but I think you should leave,"

Mandy yelled. I glanced over at her to see her face was red with anger. Mandy was normally a pretty calm person, but insulting her parents was one way to get her goat. "My father does not think of himself as high and mighty. He is a great man, even greater because he puts up so nicely with people like you."

Cindy's eyes narrowed and suddenly the Poodle Woman looked more like a cobra, venom spewing from her in the form of hurtful words. Behind her, Hilda's eyes widened not in surprise but in excited support.

"Well look at you," Cindy said. "You must be Sally Jr. You look just like your mama, but I hope you don't act like her. I hate to tell you, but your Queen Bee mama acts like a, well, it's a profane word I don't let slip out of my mouth. If I were you, I'd tell your parents to shape up their acts."

I glanced over at Mandy. By the way she looked, I was kind of glad we were currently bobbing in a pool because if we weren't, I would have to be physically restraining her.

"Cindy, I think that's enough," Sally said. Her firm tone betrayed just how upset she really was. "You should leave before things get any more heated."

"My mother is being too nice," Mandy said. "Leave or else you may need to watch your back."

"I will leave, but only because I have to get my

dinner ready," Cindy said. "Hilda, come along."

They both turned and walked out, Cindy waved her fingers in a sort of mocking goodbye. The metal gate slammed shut and the pool remained quiet.

"Oh that Cindy is just the worst," Louise finally said, slapping her hand against the water. "She better watch out or she will get what's coming to her."

"You're right," Susie said. "That park snitch will end up in a bad position one day if she keeps on like that."

"I hate to say it, but you are all right," Bill said. "That woman just does not know when to stop. She is bound and determined to keep at it until every single one of us is gone. And after she chases all of the Guys and Dolls out, she'll start on the other residents. Someone needs to stop her."

Everyone nodded their heads vigorously, which made the pool ripple up and down with little waves. As someone totally on the outside of this entire conflict, I could kind of see both sides although I couldn't say I would want to be on Cindy's side.

The Guys and Dolls did seem to be a little too exclusive. If they were making decisions that had to do with the entire park, I could see how frustrating it would be to not be involved. On the other hand, Cindy was just too black and white. The world was much more a shade of gray and, as Bill pointed out, did it really matter how many chairs he had on his deck?

The one thing I did know for sure was that Cindy seemed to be intruding in the wrong place. If she had problems with the Guys and Dolls, this was definitely not the way to go about addressing it. Looking around, everyone was glad that she was gone and seemed to agree with the vague threats being thrown around.

As a total outsider though, I was more intrigued than anything. I would have to ask Mandy's parents for more information about Cindy. I really wanted to understand more about what made her tick.

•Chapter Five•

Dinner that night was just grilling out on Bill and Sally's deck, which was a nice way to slow down a bit after the go go go pace of the rest of this day. I couldn't believe that we had just flown in that morning. I felt like I'd been in Florida for days already, but sitting on the slightly shaded deck in the Florida heat was lovely. It was absolutely wonderful, especially thinking about the piles of snow that we had left behind. Thinking about Minnesota, I realized I'd been so busy that I hadn't even messaged Max. I picked up my flip phone, opened it up, and typed out a quick hello.

I don't mean to brag, but I'm currently having a chilled glass of wine on a warm, sunny deck in a pair of shorts and flip flops. I hope your car started this morning! :P

I shut the phone as Sally sat down next to me. Bill was busy at the grill and Mandy was hovering around him, alternating between actually helping and just being in the way. Together we giggled as Mandy and Bill turned and ran right into each other as they both milled around the grill.

"I'm so glad you girls are here," Sally said. "This really is the highlight of our year. We love when Mandy comes, but this time is so great because you were able to come too."

She reached over and patted my hand. I felt so happy to be visiting them because in high school, they were second parents to me. There was also a twinge of guilt. When I left Shady Lake, I started to slowly cut ties with almost everyone. My family and Mandy were the only ones that I stayed close with.

"Sally, I'm sorry that I didn't reach out to you when I left for college," I said quietly. I had to let these feelings of guilt out. I held enough emotions inside, even now almost two years after Peter's death. I didn't want to hold that guilt inside along with it.

"Oh honey, you don't need to apologize," Sally said, taking my hand as I felt the tears well up in my eyes. "When you went to college, why in the world would you want to spend your free time calling two old, retired fuddy-duddies? I mean, you already were calling your parents."

She winked slyly at me making me giggle a bit. I set my wine glass down so that I wouldn't spill it.

"I didn't expect you to call me," Sally said. "I got all of the news I needed through Mandy and your mother and when it counted, I made sure you felt my love."

My mind flashed back to Sally's gift after Peter died. Most people sent flowers, but Sally's gift had been much more meaningful. She had sent a basket filled with things for me. Inside had been a comfortable blanket, some books and puzzle books, a pair of warm slippers that I still used, and a very expensive box of chocolates. The small card told me that she loved me and that the important thing right now was to keep soldiering on however I could through all of the emotions by taking care of myself.

Another stab of guilt ran through me when I realized I had never sent her a thank you card. I went back and forth about whether I should apologize and thank her now, but I decided to just leave well enough alone. I also had that little voice in my head telling me that my mother had most likely sent a thank you for me.

"By the way, I meant to ask you something earlier," I said, trying to shove the guilt away. "I noticed that all of the Dolls had matching pins. What is that about?"

"Oh our membership pins!" Sally said. "We wanted something that would set us apart and that people could use to identify us during park events. Now we kind of just wear them everywhere except when we're bobbin'."

I took another sip of wine. That made sense, but somehow I was hoping for a bit more of a story behind them. Oh well, not everything can have some big and grand meaning behind it.

"Oh geez, looks like I'm needed," Sally said. She grabbed her wine glass and floated towards the grill where Mandy and her father were happily bickering about whether they should cook the steaks for a few more minutes. I couldn't help but smile before I felt my phone buzz. Pulling it out of my pocket, I was happy to see a message from Max.

I wish your phone had a better camera so I could ask for a picture! But you're right, I am jealous. Maybe next time you go on a trip, I can come along. Love you.

I shivered a little bit with the thought of taking a romantic vacation with Max. Obviously we wouldn't take one down here to the Candy Cane Park but maybe somewhere nearby. Visions of beach walks and outdoor candlelit dinners flashed through my head as I took another sip of my wine. I typed a quick message back.

Love you too. Just wait till I'm able to call and fill you in on all of the gossip here at the retirement RV park. It is almost like a soap opera.

"I think I set them straight," Sally said, lowering herself back into the chair next to me. "Hopefully they won't need more sage guidance from me to finish that dinner."

"Sally, can I ask you about something?" I asked. "What is going on between Cindy and everyone else? She is so angry. Why is she like that?"

"Oh Cindy," Sally sighed. "First of all, I don't really think she is a bad person. I think that she is just bitter and when things didn't quite go her way, it really threw her for a loop. The first year when she wanted to join the Dolls, she didn't apply in a happy, want to be friends kind of way. She came charging in demanding to be let in so that she could take over because she had a bunch of ideas for how the Dolls could be run better. She actually had an entire plan where the Dolls would cease to be a social club and become more of a strictly run business that doesn't actually make money."

"But why?" I asked. "Why would she want to change the Dolls from a fun thing into something so much more clinical?"

"I'm not exactly sure, but she used to be quite a powerful business woman, you know. She started a chain of craft and hobby stores and sold them all at a very high profit. We have all assumed that she is worth quite a bit of money. To me, Cindy is a prime example that money can't buy happiness."

I took another sip of my wine and mulled that over. It made even less sense now. I figured Cindy had some tragic backstory that made her act the way she acted. The idea that she was some sort of ruthless business woman who had retired with tons of money but wanted to use her free time to take over a social club that she would rule with an iron fist was such a strange idea.

"But she managed to find herself one friend," I said. "She has Hilda, right?"

"She does have Hilda," Sally said, tipping her head towards me. "Before Cindy moved in, Hilda was a pleasant woman, but always so painfully shy that no matter how we tried to include her, she always shrunk away. If we came to the pool and she was lounging on a deck chair there, she would pack up and leave even though we would try to welcome her in to bob with us. When Cindy came, Hilda latched onto her. I'm not exactly sure why because it isn't like Cindy is nice to her, but perhaps she offers Hilda some sort of social shield. That's the only thing I can figure."

There had to be more to the story, but Sally didn't know and it wasn't like I was going to go ask Cindy or Hilda about it. Some things just might have to remain a mystery.

"One more thing," I said. I just couldn't help myself. "Cindy mentioned reporting rule breakers to the owner of the park. Does she do that often?"

Sally snorted into her glass of wine before she launched into a coughing fit. I took the glass out of her hand and set it on the side table between us. After a few minutes of regaining her composure, Sally was finally able to answer my question.

"Sorry dear, but yes," Sally said. "I would say she does it even more than 'often.' She submits a detailed list of rule breakers and all of their offenses each and every week. If she's feeling extra crabby that week, she even includes a page where she lists what the punishments should be."

"But you said the owner of the park doesn't care?" I asked.

"Tom is an excellent man who puts up with Cindy better than anyone else here," Sally said. "Probably because he doesn't actually live on site. He's able to just put up with her at the weekly meeting he holds. Each week she introduces her list of infractions and each week, Tom picks one or two to take minimal action on and we all move on with our lives."

"What kinds of infractions are there?" I asked, remembering the arbitrary rule about the number of chairs on a deck. If it was all rules like that, no wonder the owner didn't really care.

"Oh my, all sorts of things," Sally said. She looked a bit exasperated and tired. "Some of the rules make sense, like no parking on the street. All cars must be in the parking stalls or guest parking lot because the streets are so narrow that it just doesn't work. But most of the other rules were put into place by the former owner and are so picky that they just aren't worth enforcing. You're only supposed to have two potted plants on your deck, you aren't supposed to plant anything in the ground, each deck is supposed to only have four chairs on it, and you aren't supposed to have any sort of large storage container outside. Most of them are to help prevent eyesores, but I think they are more just pains in the behind."

"So why don't you all just get rid of those rules?" I asked. "You said the owner now is different."

"Unfortunately, most of them are based on city ordinances," Sally said. She took a sip of her wine and I mirrored her, still fascinated about how much drama can brew in a retirement RV park. "We wouldn't be able to get rid of the rules, so we would have to go through a big thing to put similar rules into place. It is much easier for us to just have the rules and ignore them. At least, it would be easier if we didn't have someone who was absolutely set on following each and every stupid rule."

At that moment, Cindy rounded the corner on a rickety bicycle. It looked like it had been a red bike at one time, before it had been overtaken by rust. A wicker basket was attached to the front and sticking out the top was a clipboard. There was also a childish vanity plate attached to the front that said CINDY on it. Usually I thought vanity plates were for things that a person would be really proud of, but here was one stuck to a heap of scrap metal which just made me think that the world takes all sorts of people to make it run. Cindy's hawkish eyes seemed to be scanning the neighborhood for infractions. Suddenly, a scowl appeared on her face and she stopped her bicycle, taking the clipboard out and jotting down a few notes.

"Still too many chairs on your deck," Cindy called out to us as her pen flew across the paper.

I glanced over at Sally who had a look on her face like she'd just eaten a lemon. I'd always known Sally to be sweet as pie, but I could see how much she disliked Cindy and if I was being honest, I could understand why. Sally opened her mouth, but before she could say anything, Bill piped up instead.

"Oh Cindy, if you'd like to join us in one of these contraband chairs, you are more than welcome," his voice boomed from the grill. "Or are you too busy getting ready for the dance tonight?"

"I'm much too busy to join you in your illegal reverie," Cindy snarled. "As for the dance, I will be there, but mostly I'll be making sure things don't get out of hand. Someone has to manage this park and goodness knows that Mr. Parks won't be the one to do it for fear he anger the Guys and Dolls."

The sarcasm was laid on thick as Cindy rolled her eyes. She finished writing whatever she was writing and stuck her clipboard back into her basket. Her tight, poodle-like curls bounced slightly as she got back onto her bike. She started to ride away, but she had one more thing to say.

"You just all better watch out," Cindy called over her shoulder. "Because I've been gathering evidence and soon I might have a big enough case to get everyone kicked out. And I'll start with the two of you."

As she tottered down the street on her rickety bicycle, I hoped it would wobble enough to finally fall apart. She circled at the end of the dead-end street and rode towards us one more time. I turned to look at Bill and Mandy, who were standing frozen by the grill. Thankfully, they had already turned the grill off and plated the food before Cindy came or we would have been faced with a dinner of charred food.

"You watch out Cindy," Mandy suddenly screeched. "If you aren't careful, someone's going to make sure that you get kicked out or worse!"

By this point, a few of the neighbors on the street were very obviously watching us. I couldn't blame them, of course, because between Cindy's bicycle patrol and Mandy's extra loud screaming, we were making quite the scene.

Cindy glared as she rode by before doing the international symbol for 'I'm watching you,' pointing her two fingers at her eyes and then pointing at us. Mandy made a rude gesture back, but Bill noticed and grabbed her hand, forcing it back down from where a certain finger had been waving freely in the air. Cindy stuck her nose in the air and turned onto the main road, riding out of our sight.

"Well I'm going to be honest," Sally said. "I

think that could have gone a lot better."

I nodded at her and turned to look at Mandy once again. Bill and Sally were both looking pointedly at her but Mandy was staring off into the distance, ignoring their looks like a petulant child.

"What did she mean that she's going to get you kicked out?" I asked. I had been under the impression that Cindy was mostly harmless, unable to get her ideas as to who should be punished past the park owner and the Dolls.

"The park as a whole is governed by a board that oversees all of the RV parks in the area," Bill explained as he set down the plates of food on the table. "There was a large turnover in the members of the board and Cindy has gotten quite friendly with many of them. They are of the same thought when it comes to mindless rule following and unfortunately if Cindy builds a big enough case, they can take action against the park and all of us who break all of those idiotic rules."

"What sort of action?" Mandy asked, still scowling even though the encounter with Cindy was long over.

"They can fine the park," Bill said. "They could fine Mr. Parks a lot of money and really, we would not let that happen to him. We would rather be forced out than bankrupt him. They could also start issuing tickets to us and if we ignore them, we could possibly be arrested but that would be a long time down the road."

"Long way down the road or not, that would be terrible," I said. "So it sounds like Cindy is becoming more than just an annoying pest."

"She sure is," Bill said. "But I think we need to put that out of our minds and focus on eating dinner. We have got to be going soon."

Mandy's face mirrored my confusion as we looked back and forth between Bill and Sally. They were happily scooping food onto their plates before they realized we had not been clued into the plan for the rest of the night.

"Oh I must not have mentioned it," Sally said with a smile. "We are going to a dance tonight."

Chapter Six

When Sally had said we were going to a dance, the only thing I could picture was a high school dance. In my mind I could see a darkened gymnasium with speakers blaring hip hop music, a few colored lights that danced around, and a lot of awkward encounters. Trying to fit that idea in with a bunch of senior citizens was particularly troubling to my imagination.

It all made a lot more sense when we entered the great room of the Candy Cane Palace and there were already several couples there practicing various types of square dancing, as a country western band tuned up on a little stage at one end of the room. I was immediately glad I hadn't worn the miniskirt and knotted up t-shirt that my high school self would have worn to a school dance.

The band was comprised of a handful of senior citizens. They were all dressed up in matching white button-up shirts, jeans, a red bandanna around their necks and a cowboy hat, all except for the one female member of the band. She wore a long, denim skirt while she played the fiddle.

Sally and Bill led the way as we came in the door, fielding shouts of hello, hoots and hollers at their matching outfits. Sally had on a big, poofy blue skirt that matched Bill's shirt and they both had on big white cowboy hats that had blue ribbons tied around the base. Most of the couples were dressed in similar outfits, matching each other with big skirts and fancy cowboy hats.

Mandy and I were nowhere near as fancy. We had both slipped into a sundress and some sandals, not sure what we were getting ourselves into. I was very relieved to see that there were chairs set up along the edge of the room for the spectators where I fully expected to be for the entire evening. Let's just say that I am not the most coordinated person and, seeing as I had never square danced before, I didn't foresee myself joining in the hoopla.

"Okay everyone, we are ready to start the dancing," the lead cowboy said into the microphone. "If everyone could please make their way to the floor and we will get started with some of the easier dances."

Mandy and I found some chairs on the edge of the floor and watched the dancers arrange themselves. As the country music started and the lead cowboy started to call out directions, the skirts swirled around the floor as the couples moved around the square.

I couldn't help myself, clapping along with the music and tapping my toe as the happy couples danced around the floor. Every once in a while, someone would go the wrong way resulting in a collision and the couples in that square would collapse into giggles like a bunch of children.

At one point, I saw Sally and Bill with big smiles on their face. They looked almost like two teenagers in love. I elbowed Mandy to point it out to her, but her eyes were on the entrance door, a sneer settled on her face.

Standing in the doorway to the Candy Cane Palace was Cindy with Hilda a half step behind her, never quite able to be Cindy's equal. I wondered what in the world would draw them to this dance. An atmosphere of fun and frivolity did not seem to be Cindy's cup of tea, so what reason could she have for crashing this party?

Mandy started to stand up, but I caught her arm and pulled her back down into the metal folding chair.

"What are you doing?" I asked. "Leave Cindy alone."

"I wanted to apologize," she said. The scowl on her face was unconvincing.

"Yeah right," I said. "Sit yourself back down."

Mandy leaned back and crossed her arms, once again looking like a petulant child. She was trying to avoid looking at me, but I just rolled my eyes at her. I went back to watching the dancers circle around, stepping together and apart and occasionally switching partners.

Suddenly, Louise caught my eye storming across the edge of the dance floor towards the entrance. As always, she seemed a bit awkward. Where the other dancers looked tidy and put together, Louise was just a little bit off. Her shirt was partially untucked, giving her a rumpled appearance and from what I could see, she and her husband's outfits were not at all matching.

She made her way all the way to the entrance where Cindy watched her approach with a sort of devilish glint in her eye. I had to admit that of all the people to come confront me, I would be the most amused about sweet Louise coming over. She may not be the most intimidating, but her determination was to be admired.

"I'm going to grab a cupcake," I said to Mandy. She gave a distracted nod of her head even though I could tell she hadn't heard me at all. If she had, I think she may have come with me. She couldn't stop staring at Cindy in all of her glory. Her poodlelike hair was piled high on her head and a cowboy hat was perched on top, teetering a bit as she surveyed the crowd.

The food table was located right next to the entrance, so it gave me a convenient excuse to eavesdrop on the conversation, not that I actually needed to be that close to them. The music was blaring so loudly that Louise and Cindy were practically screaming at each other.

"You better not have come to cause more trouble," Louise shouted. Her skirt was swishing from side to side as she practically vibrated with anger. "You mark my words: if you cause trouble here, you will regret it. You've ruined everything else. You aren't going to ruin this dance too."

As I grabbed a cupcake, someone brushed past my arm. I turned and saw it was Susie but when I tried to say hello, she didn't seem to hear me. It seemed she was headed towards the entrance to back up Louise.

"Oh shut it," Cindy said. "I know you feel more than a bit insecure about your place in the Dolls. And you should, because that place was rightfully mine. But you don't have to put on this sort of spectacle for everyone just to try to show your superiority."

"That's enough," Susie said as she joined them. "We all know you like to pick on those who seem defenseless, but you just try to pick on me. Your words don't hurt me and if we come to blows, I'm pretty sure I could beat you."

I took a bite of the cupcake and while I chewed up the overly sweet frosting along with the slightly dry cake, I had to admit that Susie was right. She was the most fit senior citizen I had ever seen and honestly, she was more physically fit than most of the people I knew who were my age. I'm not sure what she did to work out, but her arms were nicely toned. I had to assume a mixture of tennis and maybe a rowing machine.

Cindy still had not said a word to the odd pair of women who had confronted her. Hilda stood behind her, nervously chewing off the pink lipstick she had applied for the dance. After a moment, Hilda took hold of Cindy's sleeve and gave a small tug, backing up like she wanted to just disappear back into the night, but Cindy stood her ground.

"Ha, are you threatening me?" she said with a giggle. "That was directed towards both of you. I mean, only one of you threatened me physically but they were threats all the same. I came to enjoy the music, just like the two of you."

Cindy seemed to actually be enjoying this encounter. I was close enough to it that I could study her face and instead of being flustered by all of this attention, she seemed to be thriving on it. Cindy kept licking her lips like she was excited by the possibility of a bigger confrontation and more people watching.

As I munched on my subpar cupcake, I realized that the reason Cindy was like this was probably a lot like some of the guys who were the enforcers on hockey teams. They knew they wouldn't be the star of the show and that they wouldn't be the goal-scoring hero, but they also knew they had a place in people's hearts as almost a sort of villain.

Staring at Cindy standing in the doorway, I realized that she lived for this attention. And in that moment, I felt sad for the Poodle Woman. She had Hilda, but I got the idea that being around Hilda was a bit like being best friends with a wet sponge. Cindy must crave attention and she had definitely found a way to get more of that.

"Why are you eating a second cupcake?" Mandy said as she appeared at my side. "They are kind of gross."

I looked down and realized that I'd been so wrapped up in this situation that I had grabbed another cupcake and had already eaten a few bites of it before I even knew what was happening. At least I had taken the paper off first.

"It was part of my excuse to come over here," I said.

"That explains the first one, but not this one," she hissed.

"Well what are you doing here?" I asked. Last time I had looked at her, she had still been sitting cross-armed in the metal folding chair where I had left her.

"I came to my senses and saw that you had come over here for a better view and I couldn't let you have all the fun," Mandy said. "Besides, depending on what happens, I have a few choice words for the Dog Lady."

"Poodle Woman," I said before I became aware of the fact that I'd just become complicit in the mean nickname they called Cindy, even if her hair did look vaguely poodlelike. "I mean, not that we should call her that either because it is pretty mean when you think about it."

Mandy appeared to be thinking about it for sure but judging by the fire in her eyes, the devil on her shoulder was winning this round. I was starting to get a small glimpse of what Mandy regularly dealt with when she had to pull me back from the brink. I felt like we had somehow switched roles during this trip.

I looked back towards the door to see Cindy push between Louise and Susie into the gymnasium. Most of the square dancers seemed to still be oblivious to the scuffle that was threatening to throw down at the doors. But Cindy didn't get far into the dance because as I turned to see who else was paying attention, Mandy slipped by me and grabbed Cindy's arm.

"You need to leave," she said. "You aren't welcome here."

"Mandy!" I shouted. I could see from the wince of pain that crossed Cindy's face that Mandy was holding her arm just a bit too tight to be friendly.

"She's welcome here," Hilda squeaked as she scurried over. "She lives here in the park. You don't even live anywhere near here."

"Mandy, you need to stop," I said firmly as I grabbed her other arm. "Let her go. You're taking this too far."

I looked Mandy in the eyes and as the veil of anger slowly dropped, she loosened her grip on Cindy's arm until Cindy was able to shake herself free. Mandy's eyes filled with tears as she started to understand exactly what she had been doing.

"I could have you arrested for that," Cindy hissed. "But I might just settle for getting your parents out of this park once and for all."

"You do that and I will make you pay," Mandy screamed. "Consider that a legitimate threat to your safety."

At that moment, the band leader announced a break in the dancing and the music stopped for a moment, just in time for everyone to hear Mandy's screams. All of the dancers swiveled their heads to see what was happening, their smiles slowly melting off of their faces.

Cindy smiled a slow, evil grin once more time before she threw up her hands and turned to leave, letting Mandy's threat hang in the air as the last word. Hilda stared at Mandy for a moment, her eyes as big as dinner plates before turning to scurry after her one friend in the world.

The crowd parted as Bill and Sally walked

towards us. Both of them looked concerned, which was an odd contradiction to the fun outfits they were wearing. A single tear fell down Mandy's face as she sniffled. In a way, it was oddly reminiscent of a junior high dance now that someone was crying.

•Chapter Seven•

The upbeat music was swirling around us and the dancing had started back up, but it was not quite as joyful as before. Part of the reason was that Bill and Sally were sitting with us now on their own uncomfortable, metal folding chairs instead of leading the fun out on the dance floor. As the dancers whirled by, some of them would throw glances toward us trying to figure out if they should stop and see if they could help or just keep dancing. But Bill and Sally were a bit intimidating on top of their pedestal of being unofficial park leaders and all of the dancers instead chose to simply throw some smiles and winks towards them in a friendly, supportive manner as they spun and twirled around the dance floor.

Once Cindy and Hilda left, I put my arm around Mandy and squired her away from the fray and back to the spectator chairs with Bill and Sally following close behind. For a while, we tried to start a conversation by commenting on the dancing or some of the outfits, but soon enough we lapsed into silence. No one wanted to talk about Mandy confronting Cindy or what that could mean in the long run. We sat, frozen in place, hoping the joy around us would warm us out of our stupor.

"I think I need to get the Dolls together," Sally

said suddenly as she jumped to her feet. "We need some emotional support."

Sally and her floofy skirt swished off into the sea of dancers. I looked at Bill, but he just shrugged. I'm not really sure what the Dolls were going to be able to offer us, but maybe Sally just couldn't think of anything else to do in that moment.

Soon enough, the Dolls started to appear out of the crowd. Kathy and Karen came arm in arm in matching outfits. I wondered if their husbands had been made to match each other but then I remembered that those two might also be twins, not that the fact that they were twins meant they automatically wanted to dress alike.

Marie jingled up with more bangles up her arms than she had been wearing earlier. I wondered how many she actually owned. Behind her came Lynn, her hair still teased high to the sky. She was the only one who wasn't wearing a cowboy hat. I got the impression that her hair was her crowning glory and no hat was going to potentially ruin that.

The Dolls formed a semi-circle around us, chattering away to each other and to us even though Mandy, Bill, and I were all silent. To them, silence was simply a space to fill with small talk and petticoats.

"Has anyone seen Louise or Susie?" Sally said as she bustled back into the group. "I can't seem to find them anywhere."

All of the Dolls looked back and forth at each other, each one shaking their head in turn. Apparently Louise and Susie had gone missing. I thought back to their confrontation with Cindy. Even though it had been much quieter than Mandy's conversation, it had felt just as intense to me.

"The last time I saw them was before Mandy was talking to Cindy," Lynn finally said with shrug, her hair sprayed too stiff to move with her motion. "They both talked to her first."

"Well, let's spread out and see if we can find them," Sally said.

She snapped her fingers and the Dolls were on the move, fanning out through the crowd like they had practiced this maneuver. I could almost imagine them all sniffing the ground like a pack of bloodhounds on the case of their missing friends. I was so intrigued with watching this clique of women that I didn't notice Mandy wasn't sitting next to me anymore until Bill jumped to his feet.

"Mandy, wait," he shouted at her back.

Mandy turned and I could see now that her face was tear-streaked. The emotions she had been holding back were spilling over, unable to be contained. She looked at Bill and I and shook her head fiercely, obviously telling us not to follow her. Then she turned and ran out the double doors. I stood up next to Bill but he turned and firmly pointed his finger at me.

"You stay here," he said. "You keep the Dolls in line and I will go figure out where Mandy is going."

I opened my mouth to protest, but snapped it back shut as Bill and his cowboy hat dashed out of the gymnasium. The dancers kept whirling around and around as the Dolls dashed between them, almost a part of the dance themselves. The members of the band kept glancing at the rogue women, scowling slightly as they tried to figure out exactly what was going on. I wasn't sure of that myself.

After some time, the same five members of the Dolls reconvened around me and the two now empty chairs that had previously been occupied by Mandy and Bill. Apparently they had been unable to find the two missing members of the group.

"Aw heck, where did Bill and Mandy go now?" Sally said. "Don't tell me that we are now missing four people."

"Well kind of," I said. "Mandy got really upset and ran out, but Bill followed her. So I don't know where they are but I wouldn't exactly say they are missing."

"If we don't know where they are, I consider them missing," Marie said as she rolled her eyes, her bangles clanging together as she let out a big, shoulder-rolling sigh.

"Okay fine, they're missing," I said. "But if you all keep running around on that dance floor, I think the band leader might come down here and run you out of the dance once and for all."

"Let's go out and start searching the park then," Sally said. "Karen and Kathy, you start with Louise's place. Marie and Lynn, you head to Susie's. Tessa, you're with me. We will figure out where Bill and Mandy went."

With a sharp nod of their heads and a feeling like we should have all put our hands in and yelled 'break,' the older women all turned and practically ran out the doors back into the park, their heels click-clacking out of the gymnasium. I had to hustle to keep up with them and once again I was confronted with the fact that I really should start exercising more often.

Spilling out into the evening, I stopped short outside of the gymnasium. The other women scurried away in different directions while I took a deep breath and looked around. The sky was a dusky pink orange color and the air was still warm. Unfortunately instead of being able to enjoy this beautiful night, I had joined a roving band of elderly women investigators to find our missing friends. Sally was walking the patio outside of the Candy Cane Palace, but she quickly walked back to where I was standing.

"I don't think there's anyone out on the patio," she shouted over the sounds of the loud music. "Obviously we can see most of it and the only part we can't see is the pool area. I'll just have Bill check that when he closes up the pool later."

I thought about pointing out to her that Bill was currently missing, but decided against it. Sally took off into the park before I could say anything to her and I tried my hardest to keep up with her.

After a semi-frantic search that seemed to last for an hour but was more like twenty very intense minutes, the Dolls and I gathered back up by the Candy Cane Palace. The country music was still spilling out of the doors to the gymnasium, but none of us made any move to go back inside.

"So Louise is back at home," Sally said. "But we still can't find Susie, Bill, or Mandy. What should we do?"

"At this point I think we just have to leave them be," Marie said. "I'm sure they didn't go far. Let's just go wind up this square dance and call it a night. Tessa, you go on and take Sally home while we collect our husbands and pay the band."

I nodded and looked at Sally who, for the first time since we had arrived, seemed to be a little lost. This woman who was so used to being the head honcho wasn't sure what the next step should be. I took her by the elbow and waved goodnight to the

Dolls who shouted their well wishes as the doors to the gymnasium closed behind them.

Mandy couldn't have gone far. She and Bill were probably taking a walk or something to process her confrontation with Cindy. I just hoped they would be home soon so that Sally and I could have some peace of mind soon.

•Chapter Eight•

When morning dawned, Mandy was squished up beside me on the foldout couch bed. I had stayed up late into the night watching bad television while I waited for her to get home but sometime between when I fell asleep and now, she had found her way back. That must have meant that Bill was back too, but the door to the bedroom was closed so I assumed he was also sleeping.

Looking at the clock on the wall, it was only 6am which was way too early for me, especially after my late bedtime. But I could also feel that I was not going to be able to get back to sleep. Somehow, my body had decided it was awake. Why didn't this happen on mornings when I had to get up for work?

I crawled as delicately as I could out of the bed, trying not to disturb Mandy. The smell of coffee wafted over from the kitchenette and hit me full force. As I poured myself a cup, I could see Sally puttering around on the deck. I pushed the door open and walked through the sunroom, thankful that my pajamas were just a pair of sleep pants and a t-shirt since I didn't have anywhere private to change at the moment.

"Good morning Darling," Sally said from her chair. "I hope you slept alright on that horrible couch bed."

"Good morning," I said, sitting next to her with my steaming mug of coffee. "Yes, I slept just fine. I was so tired from everything we did yesterday! And I'm assuming by the fact that Mandy is passed out in bed that Bill must also be home?"

"Yes dear," she said. "They both got home about three hours ago."

We sat together sipping our coffees in silence. It was a beautiful, already warm morning. I just wanted to sit and soak up the sun without trying to dissect what happened the night before. Once Mandy was awake, I would pry the details out of her.

"Are you alright if I go up to the pool for an early morning workout?" Sally said, standing up from her chair. I could see the strings of her swimming suit poking out the top of her shirt. "I like to go before anyone comes to bob so that I can do some water aerobics without anyone ogling me."

"Yes, I'm fine," I said. "I can always grab a book to read or something. Really, I'm just glad to soak up some sunshine."

Sally smiled at me with a wink as she grabbed a towel off of one of the other chairs on the deck. As I watched her walk up the street towards the Candy Cane Palace, I debated going in to grab a book but the sun felt so warm that I just couldn't make myself get up out of it. Instead I closed my eyes and thought once more about taking a vacation with Max to somewhere warm.

Max and I had only made our relationship more serious in the last few weeks and since then, we saw each other every single day for at least a few minutes. Now I hadn't seen him in almost two days and I was missing him like crazy. It felt like when we were in high school and I would go to a church mission trip or he would go to sports camp. Even though I was having fun, I knew that if I let my thoughts dwell on Max the whole time the trip would drag on and on in an endlessly torturous way.

But I couldn't help myself right now. I thought about us going to a resort somewhere warm. Max and I could swim in the ocean and lounge next to the pool. Maybe we could go scuba diving or on a dolphin excursion or something equally exotic. It wouldn't really matter what we did as long as we were somewhere warm and sunny together.

Just as I was picturing a sunset dinner on the beach, a scream pierced the morning quiet. My eyes popped open and I glanced around, wondering if I had just been hearing things. It was so unexpected that I figured I had just misheard something. But another scream came and this time I was able to pinpoint that it was coming from the direction of the Candy Cane Palace.

Sally!

I jumped out of my chair just as the door from the sun room slammed open. Bill came out, his hair rumpled and wearing clashing red and yellow shirt and shorts that had obviously been thrown on in a hurry. I looked around for some shoes and spotted a pair of flip flops that I jammed my feet into.

"That's Sally screaming," Bill said, his eyes looking around in a panic. He still looked half-asleep and hoping the scream had just been part of a nightmare. "Where is she?"

"She just left for the pool," I said.

I barely got the words out of my mouth before Bill leapt down the stairs and started running towards the pool. Mandy was nowhere in sight but instead of going in to wake her, I followed Bill's lead and took off behind him towards the pool. If something had happened to Sally, I knew that Bill would need someone there with him.

Fighting my way through the bushes around the pool, I finally found the gate opening. It made it a lot easier to find when there were plenty of other residents streaming in to see what had happened.

In his haste, Bill had thrown the gate wide open and it was stuck in the bushes. We were definitely not the only people who had heard the scream. Several residents were already going in the gate and more were coming behind me. Some of them I recognized from square dancing or just seeing them around the park since I had arrived, but most of them I didn't recognize at all.

It was so early that I almost didn't recognize Cindy, who still had a head full of curlers instead of her signature hairdo. Cindy scowled at me as we both tried to squeeze in the gate at the same time and it took all that I had to not throw a scowl back at her.

Once I was in the pool area, Sally was standing next to the pool soaking wet with her face buried in Bill's chest. She was loudly crying and I realized that she was not the only one. There were so many people milling around that I didn't really know what was going. All I could see was chaos. Some of the residents were clustered together crying while others walked aimlessly around the pool area. I still couldn't tell why Sally had screamed or what was making everyone cry.

Suddenly, I felt a tug on my arm. Looking over, I realized that Cindy was starting to fall to the ground, grasping at the closest thing to her which happened to be my arm. Confused, I reached over and pulled her back to her feet but she refused to hold her own weight. I tried again, but she still just kept sliding down to the ground. Cindy's face was contorted into a look of horror, her mouth and eyes all wide open. I helped her slowly to the ground and as soon as she was settled, Cindy let out a loud, painful wail as she pointed to the pool.

I looked over at the pool and realized that in my haste, I had missed the most important thing in the pool area that morning. Everything suddenly seemed to make more sense once it registered in my brain exactly what I was looking at. Floating face down in the pool was Hilda Brown.

•Chapter Nine•

After a moment I realized that Cindy was still sitting next to my feet, gut-wrenching wails coming from deep inside of her soul. It had seemed like Cindy only saw Hilda as an underling, but it was very apparent that she cared for her deeply as a friend. Hilda had been her only friend and now she was all alone in a place where she had only made enemies.

I sank down until I was sitting cross-legged next to her, debating whether I should try to comfort her. It wasn't so much that I didn't want to make her feel better, but more that I wasn't sure she would let me try to help. Cindy's curlers bobbed back and forth as her chest heaved with sobs. I finally decided I'd rather comfort someone who didn't want it than ignore someone so obviously in pain.

As I put my arm around her shoulders, she threw a glance at me. Her lips turned down just enough to tell me that she wasn't entirely pleased, but she allowed me to give her the slightest of hugs. Each time she took in a deep breath, it never seemed to be big enough. Cindy's sobs quickly became quieter, interspersing themselves with hiccups and sniffles.

"Can I help you over to a chair?" I asked once I felt like the initial shock of seeing Hilda had worn off.

"Of course," Cindy snapped. "Anyone with any brains would have already brought me over there."

I gritted my teeth as I helped her to her feet and towards the row of chairs that sat around the perimeter of the pool. I refrained from making a comment about trying to carry her dead weight. After Peter had died and I was learning about grief, I learned that many, many different emotions can come with it. Some people will dive immediately into sadness, some will try to ignore their feelings, and others will lash out in anger. Apparently Cindy defaulted to anger.

Cindy sank down onto the pool chair and took a deep breath while she looked at the pool once again. She quickly looked away, squeezing her eyes shut. I didn't blame her for wanting to forget the sight of her best friend's body floating lifelessly in the pool.

"Can't someone get that poor woman out of the pool?" she screeched.

Everyone who had been milling around the pool immediately fell silent and looked around, wondering who had said that. Cindy stood up and pointed her wrinkled, bony finger around the pool slowly.

"I said, someone get her out of the pool," she screeched again.

"Cindy, we can't," a man said. I recognized him as being the husband of either Karen or Kathy but just as I can't tell them apart, I can't tell their husbands apart either.

"What are you talking about?" Cindy said. "Can't any of you swim without your stupid pool noodles?"

"When we called the emergency dispatchers, they told us not to move the body," the man said. "It is very obvious that Hilda is dead. Getting her out of the pool at this point won't bring her back to life."

Cindy let out another loud wail and sank back down into the pool chair. Sally made her way through the crowd to sit on the chair next to Cindy. Sally was wrapped in a towel and her hair was dripping wet.

"Cindy, I did try to get her out of the pool," Sally said quietly. "When I came in and saw her floating in the pool I screamed, but then I realized I had to try to help her. I jumped in and I was pulling her with all of my might. But she was already gone. I kept trying but then whoever called the emergency line said to leave her because a crime may have been committed and she was already gone."

"But you didn't have to leave her floating there," Cindy said in a whisper.

"I didn't want to," Sally said with a sniffle. "Bill had to pull me out of the pool because I didn't want to leave her alone."

Cindy reached over and took Sally's hand, squeezing it and letting go so fast that I almost thought I had hallucinated it. That tiny show of humanity was enough to touch me deep down in my soul, enough to bring up just a small amount of my own grief. A vision of Peter's face the last time I saw him floated through my mind before I shoved the grief back down. Now was not the time to deal with my grief. It would have to wait for later.

"Thank you," Cindy whispered.

Far away, I could hear the sirens of emergency vehicles getting closer. The sounds around the pool were getting a bit quieter as residents were floating away, both to distance themselves from death and to spread the story of what they had seen this quiet morning.

"What happened?"

I jumped as Mandy appeared through the crowd at my side. I had written her off as dead asleep when she hadn't come out with Bill. And I had to admit that with all of the craziness of the situation, I had kind of forgotten that she was still back in the camper.

"What happened?" Cindy said. As soon as she saw Mandy, something inside of her changed. Cindy's face was raw with emotions, but now the grief had been replaced with pure rage. "You should know what happened. You did this!"

Mandy looked around confused, obviously having missed the dead body floating in the pool just like I had. The rest of the hubbub was a bit distracting. I nodded my head toward the pool in as small of a gesture as I could manage. Mandy turned and her face drained of color as she saw Hilda's dead body floating in the pool.

"What happened to Hilda?" Mandy said in a whisper.

"What happened was that you shoved her in the pool and she drowned," Cindy yelled.

"Hold on," Bill said, striding over from where he had been working crowd control by the edge of the pool. "You can't just go around accusing people of murder, Cindy."

"I'm not accusing just anyone, Bill," Cindy said. She stood up, poking her bony finger at Mandy. "I'm accusing the woman who threatened Hilda and I just last night. And if you'd take a look at the pool, you would notice that your daughter left a big old clue right next to the body."

"I didn't do this," Mandy protested.

But I spotted something else floating in the pool that my eyes had glanced over before. Next to Hilda's body was a big yellow pool noodle that clearly had the name MANDY written on it in black marker. That didn't bode well for Mandy who had been loudly heard threatening the deceased and her friend just the night before.

I walked back to where Mandy was still

protesting, now trying to explain through tears that she had simply forgotten her pool noodle the day before and that she would never hurt someone. The entire time, Cindy's wrinkled face was drawn up like she had just sucked on a lemon.

"Mandy, of course we don't think you did this," I said. "Why don't you tell us where you went yesterday after you left the dance and that should prove that you didn't do it. After all, this must have happened between the square dance last night and this morning when Sally came down here. If you account for your time, we will be able to prove for sure that you didn't do this."

Mandy's face quickly darkened to a shade of red and she glanced at her father, who held her gaze. They were definitely trying to tell each other something but whatever they were communicating, I couldn't understand it.

"You need to decide what to say, Mandy," Bill said after a moment. "I'll stand behind you either way."

I shot a glance at Sally, but she looked just as bewildered as I was. What in the world had Bill and Mandy been doing last night while they were out so late? I had to get to the bottom of this, but I knew I wouldn't be able to do it here in public.

"I don't owe her anything, especially any sort of alibi," Mandy said, narrowing her eyes at Cindy.

'But I will say one more time, I did not do this."

A group of police officers and some paramedics pushing a stretcher raced through the gate opening. Cindy hopped up out of her chair and yelled towards them.

"Hey, come on over here," she said, waving her arms over her head. "This is the person who killed Hilda. Her name is Mandy and she is right here."

Two of the police officers shot a look at each other before heading towards us. I had a feeling that this was not going to go well.

•Chapter Ten•

"Tell me one more time what happened last night," the police officer said in a monotone.

Mandy's tear streaked face looked up at him as she once again told the very shortened version of what had happened. The problem, of course, was that her version still didn't actually contain any sort of alibi for the time of Hilda's death.

"Well, we had a little confrontation at the dance," Mandy said as Cindy snorted her disgust in the background. "I got upset and left and my dad chased me. We were together until about three o'clock when we came back to the camper and fell asleep. I woke up and realized everyone was gone. When I went out on the deck to find where they went, I just followed the crowds who were headed this way."

The two police officers nodded their heads. The one officer was extremely tall and had to bend down every once in a while when Mandy got quiet because otherwise his ears were too far away to hear her. His name badge said his last name was Mendoza. The other officer was the kind of person that completely blended into a crowd. There was nothing super distinctive about him versus any of the park residents who were around except for the fact that he was at least twenty years younger and currently dressed in a police officer's uniform. His name badge read Johnson, which was so mundane that it fit him just perfectly. Together, they made an extremely odd pair.

Mandy had told them this same story with varying levels of detail at least four times so far and each time they nodded at her and then looked at each other. I'm sure they were trying to figure out exactly what they should do. Mandy didn't have a complete alibi and unfortunately, there was evidence that pointed to her. Plus it didn't help that Cindy had spent the first two retellings of Mandy's story squawking that Mandy was the killer any time Mandy paused to take a breath. One of the police officers had finally escorted her out of the pool area under the guise of having her show him to Hilda's home.

"Okay ma'am," Officer Johnson said. "Now I'm going to ask you to please give Officer Mendoza and I a moment to speak with each other in private while we consider our next steps. I'll need you to stay right here in this chair."

Mandy nodded and the two officers stepped away, walking to the end of the kidney shaped pool where they were close enough to keep an eye on us but far enough away that we couldn't hear what they were saying.

Bill and Sally were sitting on the lounge chair

on the other side of Mandy. After helping the officers escort all of the lookie-loos out of the pool area, they had staked out their place next to their daughter as a show of support. Mandy looked like she wanted to cry, but I don't think she had any tears left in her. Her cheeks were wet with all of the tears she had already cried that morning.

"What do you think they are talking about?" Mandy said. "What are they going to do with me?"

"I'm not gonna lie," Bill said. "This isn't looking very good for you, Princess."

He reached out and grabbed Mandy's hand. Sally reached out and took Mandy's other hand. I think if I had been with anyone else, I would have felt extremely awkward. But Bill, Sally, and Mandy were my second family and I wasn't surprised in the least when Mandy dropped her father's hand and grabbed mine.

For a moment, love seemed to flow between all four of us and my affection for them grew even more. Even though we were sitting next to the pool on a warm, Florida mid-morning, I shivered a little bit. I had a horrible feeling in the pit of my stomach that our vacation was going to turn out to be not much of a vacation at all.

The two officers came back around the pool to where we were sitting. Officer Mendoza's face was all scrunched up like he wasn't sure what he should say to us. Officer Johnson's face was almost blank, but I think that was just how he normally looked.

"Uh Miss, we are going to have to take you to the station with us," Officer Mendoza said after staring at us for a little longer than was comfortable. "Your family can follow in their car if they would like, but right now we will need to take you into custody for questioning. You are not under arrest because we are still trying to determine what caused this woman's death."

Mandy's face crumpled before she hid it behind her hands, her body wracked with sobs. Sally immediately covered Mandy in the sort of hug that only a mother can give. I felt like I should give Mandy a hug too, but I just couldn't. I felt frozen in confusion.

"Wait a minute," I said. "How do you even know that this is a murder? Maybe Hilda just had a horrible accident. What if she just fell into the pool by accident?"

"We can't say much," Officer Mendoza said. "But there are signs of a struggle."

As I sat unmoving, my thoughts were racing a million miles a minute. Obviously Mandy couldn't have done this and that was glaringly obvious to anyone who had ever met her. But to strangers, she did threaten both Hilda and Cindy last night, her pool noodle was found floating next to the body and worst of all, she wouldn't give an alibi for the time of the murder.

Max. I needed to call Max. He would know what to do. He could tell me the best way to deal with this.

But as I reached for my phone, I realized that Mandy was already standing up and starting toward the pool gate with the two officers.

"Mandy, do not say anything until we get you a lawyer," Bill called. "We know you are innocent, but we want to make sure they can't set you up."

Mandy turned back, her eyes open wide. Tears were still streaming down her cheeks. She nodded at us and as she disappeared through the gate, Sally collapsed onto the pool deck beside my chair. She had stayed strong as long as she needed to but now that Mandy was out of sight, she let her emotions flow. I bent down and wrapped my arms around her, hoping I could be some sort of comfort. Of course I can't replace Mandy, but I could be here for her mother while she couldn't be.

"I'm so sorry," I said, not knowing exactly what else to say.

"What if we can't prove she didn't do it?" Sally said. "We know she didn't, but how do we prove that to them?"

"I'm not sure, but the first thing we are going to do is get her a lawyer," Bill said. "No matter what I don't want the police to interrogate her and twist her words around."

"Why don't we head back to the RV?" I suggested. "My phone is back there and I'm going to try calling Max. He should be able to tell us what we should do."

Bill grabbed Sally's arm and helped pull her to her feet. He put his arm around her and steered her to the gate as I followed close behind.

Once we were through the gate, I let Bill and Sally continue on towards the RV while I shut the gate to the pool. I took one last look around, begging anything to jump out at me that I could use to prove that Mandy didn't do it but the pool looked just as it had all morning.

I ducked under the police tape that was strung around all of the bushes around the pool area. I would find something to help Mandy. There is no way I would let her take the fall for this.

•Chapter Eleven•

Back at the RV, I got my phone and headed outside onto the deck to call Max. Sally was laying down in her bed while Bill was making calls to find a good lawyer for Mandy. I didn't want them to hear me having to explain the entire situation to Max, especially Sally who had been through enough this morning. As someone who has stumbled across more dead bodies than I ever thought I would, I can personally attest to the unpleasantness.

I sat down in one of the chairs, basking in the sun for a moment before I flipped open my phone. I kind of wished I had a smartphone because then I could video call Max and be able to see his handsome face instead of just a plain old phone call. But I knew that getting a flip phone instead had been one of the best things I had done to simplify my life.

After losing Peter, there were a lot of things I reevaluated about my life. I realized I needed to simplify my life because almost everything I once thought of as so important had suddenly changed. Social media was one of those things, so I downgraded to a flip phone so that I wasn't even tempted to get back on social media.

There were some times like this, however, where I really saw the inconvenience of it. I decided I shouldn't be so smug about my 'dumbphone.' Instead I hit Max's name and waited through the rings for him to answer.

"Hey Sweet Thing," he said. "How's Florida treating you?"

My face instantly opened up with a big dumb grin that I was glad no one was around to see. He had been calling me Sweet Thing since we were in high school and it never lost it's ability to melt my heart. Sometimes the simplest things were the most important in a relationship like this.

"Hey Max," I said, before I realized that this call would need to be a lot more business-like for what was actually happening here in Florida. It felt a little weird being cutesy with my boyfriend while my best friend was sitting in the police station being accused of murder. "Actually, I don't have time for a lot of chit-chat because something happened."

"What happened? Are you alright? Where are you at?"

Max's voice instantly shifted into the deep, serious baritone of Officer Max Marcus wanting all of the details of what happened, but just the facts please. Once he turned on his law enforcement self, he couldn't switch it back off until he knew that he had sufficiently helped with whatever was going on.

"I'm alright, but I'm afraid Mandy may be in a lot of trouble," I said.

I explained the entire situation to him, starting
with the confrontation with Hilda and Cindy at the
pool yesterday, going through the fight at the dance
followed by the disappearances, and ending with
Sally finding Hilda in the pool this morning. I ended
by explaining Cindy trying to lay the blame on
Mandy and the few pieces of evidence that may not
be helping the situation. At the end of the story, I took
a big deep breath and tried to do some of the yoga
breathing I had learned at the one class Mandy had
dragged me to at the community center. Maybe I
should give that class another try when we went back
to Shady Lake.

"Okay, well this isn't the best situation for
multiple reasons, especially for Trevor," Max said
after giving me a moment to breathe. "But it also isn't
terrible. So far, the police don't have anything
physically tying Mandy to Hilda's death. Sure the
pool noodle was there, but numerous eyewitnesses
saw you both at the pool yesterday. And yes, her fight
with the ladies isn't great because it sets up an
amazing motive along with the fact that she won't
give an alibi, but I don't think she's got to turn in her
clothes for a jumpsuit just yet."

I could almost hear Max's sly smile on the
other end of the line. Leave it to him to try and add a
little humor into something that seemed so dire. On
one hand, I wanted to slap him but I had to give him

credit for trying to make me feel a little better so that I could think a little more rationally.

"This is serious Max!" I said, but I couldn't help but let out a small chuckle. Mandy had a great sense of style and I had a hard time imagining her willingly put on a prison jumpsuit. "Bill is getting a lawyer for her so that the police can't totally run her over but if I know Mandy, I know that she is strong enough that they won't be able to fool her into saying anything dumb."

"Say what you will but police officers can be handsome, clever devils," Max said. There was that grin coming through the telephone line again. Between that and the warm sun I was basking in, I felt rejuvenated and ready to fight for Mandy.

"Okay, I should go figure out what I can do to help Mandy next," I said.

I was about to say good-bye when I ran back through what Max had said and realized there had been something that hadn't made much sense. He had made some good points about the state of the police investigation, but why was it especially bad for Trevor? Sure he loved Mandy, but I didn't think he was an overly emotional man.

"You mentioned Trevor," I said. "Maybe you could be the one to call and tell him about what is going on? After all, you are back in Shady Lake with him. He might need someone to help him out. You know, someone that could bring over a pizza and distract him with a card game or movie or whatever in the heck two guys do when they hang out together."

"Umm, about that," Max said. He hemmed and hawed for a bit, making stalling noises.

"Something's up, spit it out," I said.

Normally, I would feel pretty impatient with this kind of thing, but sitting on a deck in the warm sun was putting me in a good mood. I must have replenished all of the vitamin D I'd been previously lacking from living in Minnesota in the winter.

"I wasn't supposed to tell anyone," Max said. "He only needed me to get him to the airport without paying a bunch of money to park his car up there for a few days. But it's a little too late for that."

"Airport?" I asked. Now I was really confused. "What are you talking about? Did Trevor go on a different vacation? That fink! He said he couldn't get the time off to join us down here in Florida."

"He's actually in Florida," Max said. "He was going to surprise Mandy along with her parents and you. And that's not all..."

Max let out a big exhale. I could tell he was wondering if he should tell me the rest, but I could almost guess it by now. There was only one big thing that Trevor would actually get off of his lazy butt and plan a big, romantic surprise for.

I was about to just blurt out my thoughts when Max decided he had to confide the secret in me.

"He came down as a surprise," Max said. "Trevor wanted to propose to Mandy during her trip to Florida."

•Chapter Twelve•

I did a quick check-in on Bill and Sally, but they were both still where I had left them. Sally was resting and Bill had found a lawyer and was now filling him in over the phone on the pertinent details of what happened. I grabbed a can of pop from the fridge and walked back out to the deck.

Trevor and I didn't have the greatest relationship. Don't get me wrong, it had come a long way since I moved back to Shady Lake but I still had a hard time not seeing him as the skaterboy slacker that he used to be. It didn't help that while he and Mandy had somehow maintained a long-term, monogamous, non-marriage relationship for the past twelve years, he had been slow to develop in all other areas in his life. He had kind of stumbled into a full-time job and he lived with Mandy in a nice apartment above the Donut Hut, but only because they lived there for free.

But I had to give him credit now because he was finally taking steps to improve his life and become more of an adult than an overgrown teenager. So now I was pretty neutral about him, but I still can't say that I like him. I just sort of, a little more than before, approve of him dating my best friend.

I took a deep breath and found Trevor's name

in my contact list. I had no idea what I was going to say during this phone call. The only thing Trevor and I had in common was Mandy, so I figured I should just make sure that I focus on her.

"Hi Mandy," Trevor said, practically shouting into the phone. I had to actually pull the phone away from my ear. I'm not sure if he thought he had to shout to cover up any background noise, but unless someone was yelling 'I'm in Florida' or something behind him, it wasn't like I'd be able to ascertain that he wasn't in Shady Lake if I didn't already know. "What's up? How's the weather in Florida?"

I rolled my eyes. Trevor had no idea how to play it cool, apparently. But then I remembered why he was here in Florida in the first place I had to smile a little.

"Trevor, stop the charade," I said. "I know you are here in Florida."

"What do you mean?" he said. Trevor's voice was quivering and he seemed to be debating whether to be upset that I knew or keep pretending that he was back in Shady Lake. He decided to try to play the Minnesota card a little longer. "It's like super cold here in Shady Lake today so I figure you guys are having a great time in Florida today. Since I'm definitely not there."

I let out a long sigh and made absolutely no attempts to try to hide it under my breath. Trevor was just trying to make sure his surprise remained a surprise, which it would because I had an even bigger surprise for him. Unfortunately my surprise was not a good one.

"No really Trevor, I have something really important to tell you," I said. "It is something you definitely need to know since you are down here too. Mandy was taken into custody by police."

"What?" he yelled, somehow even louder than his nervous volume from before. "Tessa, did you get her into trouble? Did you guys go out last night and get into trouble? Why aren't you in custody then?"

Wow, here I thought that my bad feelings toward Trevor were immature of me but the bad feelings appear to go both ways even after I had previously helped Trevor out of a jam. I guess I couldn't blame him because as harsh as it was for him to assume that I had gotten Mandy in trouble, my view of him as a man-child was just as harsh.

"No, it's worse," I said. I tried to remain quiet to convey the seriousness of the situation to him, even though the anger he directed at me was making me ball up my fists in frustration. "There was a murder here at the RV park and somehow Mandy has been blamed."

The other end of the line went silent. All I could hear was very quiet breathing as Trevor took in what I had just said. It was shocking news; Mandy was the last person who would commit a murder.

"Now please admit that you are in Florida so that we can get together and I can tell you what happened," I said. I was getting really tired of telling this story, but I'd have to tell it at least once more to Trevor.

"Okay fine, I'm in Florida," he said. "But I'm not telling you why."

It was statements like these that backed up my certainty that no matter what, Trevor would always be a man-child. But I needed to focus on helping Mandy right now.

"I'm staying at the Palm Tree Motel right next door to the park," he said. "I have a rental car, so I'll drive over there."

"See you soon," I said.

I snapped the phone shut before Trevor could say anything else, but it vibrated in my hand as soon as it was shut. Thankfully it had been in my hand or I wouldn't have seen I had a message for a while. The button to silence the phone was prominently displayed on the outside of the phone which meant it was always being pushed by accident and I was forever missing calls and texts. Just another reason a smartphone may be a good idea for me to consider.

Popping the phone back open, I was a little surprised to see a message from my mother. Did she somehow know that something had happened? But after reading it, it was just a coincidence. Perhaps she could tell something was happening. Mom intuition.

Haven't heard from you yet and wanted to check up on you. How's Florida? How are Bill and Sally? Tell them I need them to come down to visit soon. Love and kisses xo

Should I tell her what was happening over text message? I was tired of telling the story, especially all of the parts where Mandy kind of looked guilty. I decided to be truthful, but vague because she would know if I was lying, but I didn't feel like telling her the whole story until it was over.

It was okay, but there's been a murder in the RV park. Mandy is with the police being questioned so Bill and Sally are a bit distraught, but I'll pass on your message a bit later.

Right away, my phone buzzed with an answer. My mom had been an early adopter of the smartphone and could text faster than my high school brother Tank or any of his young friends.

I hope you don't mean they are thinking Mandy did it. If that's the case, I sure hope you have your investigative pants on and are getting her out of there. Either way, stay safe. I love you.

After texting back my love, but giving her no more information about the situation, I took a few sips of my pop from the cold can and thought about how surprised I was with my mother's message. Usually she strongly discouraged me to not investigate when these kinds of things happened. I guess when I wasn't in Shady Lake where people could scoff at her weird daughter for chasing down murderers, she was a lot looser with her rules.

●Chapter Thirteen●

I had only been able to sip my way through a quarter of my pop can before I spotted a fancy red convertible driving slowly through the park with a very out of place Trevor at the wheel. I usually thought of a convertible as being driven by a man in a suit or at least a very formal polo shirt with expensive sunglasses on.

Trevor was dressed in a graphic t-shirt that I'm sure Mandy bought for him because it was one step above his normal shirt with a modern design on it instead of some juvenile cartoon character. His hair was dark and shaggy, but not in a stylish sort of way. It was long in a sort of 'I forget to go get haircuts' kind of way. I decided I should advise him to get a haircut before he proposed to Mandy, but the ache in the pit of my stomach reminded me that Mandy might not get this proposal.

He pulled into guest parking and carefully locked the car before climbing out, apparently not thinking about the fact that it seemed a bit futile to lock the doors of a convertible since anyone could come along and unlock them. But I had to give him some credit for springing for a really, really cool rental car while he was here.

Trevor started slowly scanning the RVs as he

walked, trying to figure out where to go so when I saw him look in my direction, I gave him a little wave. He nodded and picked up the pace, not even bothering to take the stairs when he got to the deck. He was tall enough that he climbed immediately to the top one and plopped himself down in the seat next to me. Instead of slouching back into his normal posture, he was sitting straight up on the edge of his seat.

"Tell me what happened with Mandy," he said.

Trevor's voice was shaking, but he looked me straight in the eye with such a sincere look that I knew he was trying his hardest to stay strong so that he could help Mandy. It was times like these where I realized that he really, truly loved Mandy instead of seeing her as a breadwinner maid who also functioned as a stand-in mother for the man-child.

I launched into the story again, telling him every single detail I could think of because I thought he deserved it. He listened intently, trying to hide his anxiety about everything by fidgeting around and cracking his knuckles. Once I was finished, he collapsed back into his chair, his body deflating like a balloon.

"Oh man," he said quietly. "What do we need to do to get her out?"

"That's the problem," I said. "I'm not exactly sure."

"How can you not be sure, Miss Investigator?" he said. It was a bit forceful before he realized that I was not the person he needed to be upset with. "Sorry, I meant more that you've done, like, investigating before and can't you just do that again?"

"The problem is that in Shady Lake, I know the town and the people and I have Max at the police station to help me out a little," I said. "Here I don't have any of that. It's just me, myself, and I."

Trevor just sat and stared off into the distance. I took a drink of my pop and instantly felt a little guilty because even though I didn't technically live here, I felt like I should have at least offered him a drink. Instead I tried not to break the silence with any noisy drinking.

Outside of the bubble of emotions that was around the RV, life was moving on as normal. Every once in a while someone would go by, usually on foot or riding on a bicycle or in a golf cart. As they went by, they would turn and look in our direction, giving us a little wave and a small smile and then immediately turn to talk to the other people they were with, obviously chewing the fat over what had happened as if someone somewhere in the park had not already heard the news. Now I understood why Bill and Sally might not want to hang out on the deck today.

"Let's team up, Tessa," Trevor said. "I can help

you out with the investigation. I mean, maybe my work as an emergency dispatcher will come in handy. Besides, obviously I can't do what I came here to do."

Yeah, I'm sure at some point we might need to know how to operate a computer-based telephone switchboard while investigating a drowning. But he had a point that he had a lot of free time on his hands since he couldn't spend it with Mandy, although I could do without the exaggerated eyebrow raising that he was using to try to convey to me that I needed to help him keep his secret.

"Tessa, can you come in here?" Sally said as the screen door to the sun room slammed open. She stopped dead in her tracks and blinked her eyes a few times at the sudden appearance of a second person on the deck.

"Hello Miss Sally," Trevor said, standing up and striding over to her. He wrapped her in a big hug and I could see her embracing him back. I had to admit I was a little surprised by the display of affection, but I was glad that they seemed to have a good relationship.

"Come on into the sun room and tell me what in the world you are doing here," Sally said, bustling through the screen door and giving it a shove for Trevor to catch. She yelled into the RV as she entered. "Bill come out here and see who showed up."

I followed them in and by the time I was in the

sun room, Sally had already slipped into hostess mode. She was over at the bar collecting cans of pop and snacks on a tray that she carried over and set on a small table next to a few chairs. I wanted to stop her from having to play host, but it seemed like the one thing that was able to pep her up a little bit in this horrid situation.

Trevor and I each took a seat next to the tray loaded with snacks. There was fancy cheese and crackers along with the kind of olives that don't come in a can. The sight of it made my mouth water and I realized I hadn't eaten yet today, unless the can of pop I drank somehow counted. Would it be more rude to eat the food while everyone was emotionally distraught or to refuse the food that Sally put out for us? I debated back and forth in my head, but Trevor started to put together a plate of food, so I helped myself without helping myself too much.

The door to the RV opened and Bill shuffled out, looking exhausted. It had been almost two hours since we came back to the RV and I would bet he had spent that entire time on the phone. He stopped dead in his tracks, realizing Trevor had somehow joined us.

"How in the world did you get here so fast?" Bill said. "I mean, even with the first flight out of Minneapolis, I didn't think you'd be able to get here today."

"I was actually, kind of already here," Trevor

said, looking down at the floor. "But if I come clean and tell you guys why, you have to promise to keep it a secret."

"Of course, sweetheart," Sally said. She leaned forward and patted Trevor's hand. "You know we love you and you can trust us."

Trevor's chin dropped to his chest and he mumbled something down towards the plate of food he had set on his lap. Even though I was right next to him, I couldn't understand a word he said although I already knew what he was trying to say.

"Speak up," Bill said. "Nothing else will shock us today."

I practically held my breath while I waited for Trevor to tell them why he was really in Florida. Did they know anything about his plan? I popped another olive in my mouth as I looked back and forth between Sally, Bill, and Trevor's faces. Trevor finally cleared his throat and spoke up.

"Remember that time that I asked you for Mandy's hand in marriage?" Trevor said. "Well I came down here to surprise her by proposing."

I watched Sally and Bill's faces to see their reactions. Sally looked confused, her eyebrows knitted together and her mouth slightly open. Bill on the other hand had a stone face and no matter how much I searched it, I just couldn't read what he was thinking. I munched on a cracker as I looked for anger, sadness, happiness, anything I could put a label to. But if anything, I only saw a small amount of confusion.

"You asked me for Mandy's hand over five years ago," Bill finally said. "Forgive me, son, but I figured you had just decided not to propose to her. Mandy always seemed happy being with you, so it didn't bother me. I guess I'm just a little confused."

"Oh hush Bill," Sally said. "Trevor, you and Mandy have always lived life at your own pace and if you are both ready to take that step, then you know that we both support you totally and completely. But I'm assuming that Tessa told you what has happened with our beautiful Mandy?"

A tear ran down Sally's cheek. Bill stood up and walked behind her chair, covering her slim shoulders with his large, strong hands. Sally sniffled a few times before reaching up and patting one of Bill's hands.

"Yes, Tessa told me all about it," Trevor said. "And we made the decision to team up to get Mandy out of there. Tessa has solved stuff before and I'm sure I have something useful to offer to the investigation."

This time, I didn't even feel the urge to roll my eyes. Was I become a bit soft towards Trevor? I guess that is a good thing if he's finally going to marry my best friend.

"What a great plan," Sally said. "With you two gumshoes on the case, Mandy will be out in no time."

I tried to squash down my feelings of certainty and replace them with Sally's positivity. I certainly hoped that we could get Mandy out soon.

•Chapter Fourteen•

After Trevor revealed his plan, we finished up the snack tray. Well, mostly Trevor finished the snack tray with a little help from me. Bill and Sally were still too upset to eat but they did seem to perk up when Trevor said he and I were going to work together to get Mandy out of her predicament.

The first thing I had to do was one of the things that I was dreading the most. I had to talk to Bill to see if he would tell me Mandy's alibi. I knew I would be fighting a losing battle. Mandy was his pride and joy, the apple of his eye. If she was so dead set on not revealing what they had been doing, Bill may as well slap a piece of duct tape over his mouth.

I waited to see if we would come to a natural breaking point where we could naturally float to that conversation, but one never seemed to materialize. Finally, I decided to just jump in and tell them exactly what I needed to happen. I slapped my hands on my legs, causing Sally and Trevor both to jump.

"Since I am the unofficial lead investigator, I am going to tell you what I need to do first," I said. "Bill, I'm going to need to talk to you."

"I think she means that she and I both have to talk to you," Trevor supplied helpfully.

"Yes, obviously I mean both of us," I said, not

really meaning both of us. But if dragging Trevor along with me might help in any way, I supposed I would just have to get used to it. "That means that we need Sally to go inside so that we can talk in private."

"Anything you need to ask me, you can ask in front of her," Bill said. He puffed up his chest, putting on a macho act that made my face start to involuntarily pull up into a sneer. I didn't think Bill was trying to use it as a way to try to be the alpha in this situation, but I also didn't think he realized that it made him seem like a giant jerk.

He was just trying to show that he and Sally were a pair and they didn't keep any secrets from each other. And as admirable as that was, it also was totally unhelpful. If Bill and Mandy had been doing something bad, Sally would be the last person Bill would want to admit that to. He would go to the ends of the world for Mandy.

"I know, Bill, but we really need to talk to just you," I said. "We will talk to Sally separately as well, just not right now."

Bill started to protest, but Sally stood up and put her hand up. She smoothed the front of her dress, which was still just the swimsuit coverup she had thrown on this morning before knowing what the day would hold. She still somehow managed to look elegant in it.

"Knock off the macho, Bill," she said, in the

reproachful way that only a loving wife can scold her husband. "The police won't let me sit in on the interview. Tessa and Trevor shouldn't either."

Sally started to put all of the dirty dishes on the tray and I bent down to help her, but before I could do much she had already swooped the tray out of our way and floated into the RV. A minute after the door closed, I heard the kitchen sink start to fill up with water and a radio click on with music to drown out anything we might say. I had to hand it to Sally because if it had been me in her shoes, I would have been putting one of those drinking glasses to the RV wall, trying to hear what was being said out in the sun room.

Trevor and I were already sitting next to each other and I motioned for Bill to sit in the chair opposite us. He hesitated for a moment before giving in and sitting down slowly, purposefully in the chair. Bill was a tall man and while most people start to droop or even shrink as they age, Bill was still as tall and imposing as he had been when I was a kid.

"I guess the first thing I was wondering about was your job as the keeper of the pool," I said. "What does that entail exactly? Weren't you supposed to close up the pool yesterday?"

"Somehow I was deemed the keeper of the pool," Bill said before clearing his throat. "But, uh, last night I didn't get the chance to do my job. Every night, I go up there around 10 or so to close up the pool. I get out any late-night swimmers, make sure that everyone has cleaned up and make a note if anyone has left their things there. I also sometimes check the chemical levels and call for pool guys to come."

"Is it usual for you to skip out on doing your duties as keeper of the pool?" I asked.

Bill cleared his throat again, obviously a bit embarrassed at being called out on his shortcoming. He shifted in his seat a little bit, moving from side to side. He was a proud man and it looked like it pained him to admit his mistakes.

"No, it isn't usual," Bill said. "Actually, last night marks the first time I didn't go to close the pool."

He paused for a moment and Trevor opened his mouth like he was going to say something, but I silenced him with a small swat on the arm. One thing I learned from my true crime infatuation is that sometimes you just have to let people talk and that means that sometimes you wait out an awkward silence instead of filling it up with chatter.

"I guess I should also tell you that sometimes when I go to close the pool, I do let people stay to swim," Bill admitted. "If it is someone I know I can trust to close the padlock on the gate when they go out, I let them stay. Then all I have to do is go open up the pool the next morning, although usually I send the key with Sally when she goes to do her morning swim."

I let that sink in. So even if he had gone to close the pool last night, it wouldn't have really mattered because depending on who he found there, Bill may have let them stay. I wasn't sure it meant anything, but I think the fact that Bill sometimes let people overstay their welcome at the community pool may mean that the killer would be someone who knew that. If he showed up to close the pool and found a friend, he may have just walked back to the RV without even taking a peek at who else was in the pool area.

I only had one other question that I needed to ask Bill and it was one that I knew he probably wouldn't answer. But I could always hope that he would understand why I needed the answer.

"Bill, you and I were together for most of the morning today," I said. "But what I really want to hear about was last night."

"You know I can't tell you where Mandy and I went, Tessa," Bill said slowly. He folded his hands in his lap. From the true crime stuff I read, I knew that's supposed to be a sign that he was guarding something. Which, of course there was because he wouldn't say anything about Mandy's alibi. Sometimes the helpful things I learned from true crime podcasts weren't actually all that helpful in real life.

I nodded, giving myself a minute to think. Glancing at Trevor, I was thinking it would be a great time for him to actually be helpful and think of a way to get Bill talking, but instead Trevor was just sitting there bouncing his knee like a high-school kid who couldn't wait for school to end for the day.

So even though I had been roped into working as a pair, I was starting to think that I'd mostly have to go this alone. Getting upset or loud or even forceful wouldn't work on Bill. He was a man who was used to taking control of the situation. I needed to make sure I kept my cool. I decided there was only one way I might get him to talk: Mandy. It seemed a bit counter-intuitive since she was also his reason not to talk, but it was all I had.

"Mr. Bill, if you want us to help Mandy, you need to tell me what you and Mandy were doing last night," I said. "Telling me what she was doing, even if she still might get in a little trouble for it, is the best way for us to clear her name."

"I can't tell you," he said. "You'll just have to find some other way to exonerate her. But Tessa, I do have to go because I need to go meet Mandy's lawyer at the police station. I'm hoping that while I'm helping her in that way, that you can do this detective thing and help her here."

Bill stood up and waited a beat to see if we would try to stop him. Trevor and I stayed seated, letting him go. There was no way we could force him to stay and really, there was nothing else we needed from him. He started to walk towards the door to the RV but stopped halfway there, turning back around to face us.

"Tessa, I hope you know that I'm not doing this to be difficult. I want what is best for Mandy and by golly, I think you can definitely help her out."

And then he was gone, opening the door of the RV to let him in while letting out the chorus of some catchy song on the radio. I sat for a moment and wondered what he and Mandy could have done that they needed to cover up.

"We didn't learn anything from that," Trevor said, making me almost jump out of my seat.

I had almost forgotten he was there. So far, he hadn't been of any help at all except in the destruction of the snack tray. I supposed I could thank him for his work on that since my waistline did not need to take the brunt of it.

"Yes, thank you for your astute observation," I snarked. "It would have been a bit better if you had, oh I don't know, said or done something to help the situation?"

Trevor looked at me from under his dark, shaggy hair with that stupid blank look on his face

110

and I suddenly realized why high school teachers aged so fast. I couldn't imagine dealing with this all day long. Technically, at least the high school students had the excuse of age while Trevor was twelve years past being an adult.

I could feel that my face was getting red with the anger I was trying to hold in, but it all washed away when I realized that there were tears in Trevor's eyes.

"I'm sorry, Tessa," Trevor said quietly. "I just keep thinking of Mandy and how scared she must be and how this trip was supposed to be full of happy memories instead of whatever this is turning out to be."

He started to quietly cry. I wasn't sure how I was supposed to comfort him. Trevor and I hadn't even hardly texted each other in the years we had known each other, but should I give him a hug? Instead of a full-on hug, I simply slipped my arm around his shoulders and squeezed. I could feel his thin, bony shoulders as he collapsed forward, his face in his hands. I patted his back as he silently cried.

After a moment, he sat back up and swiped at his tear-streaked cheeks with the back of his hand. After a few more sniffles, he jumped to his feet and started striding to the door.

"Come on Tessa," Trevor said. "We have work to do."

Just then, a scream came from outside of the trailer. I closed my eyes for a second, which was just long enough to send up a quick thought that I really didn't want to deal with a second dead body today. Then I charged out the door, prepared to face down a murderer.

•Chapter Fifteen•

I didn't find a dead body outside of the RV, but what I did find was something much worse: Cindy was at the end of the street, yelling her head off in such a screechy manner that I couldn't understand a word that she was saying. She was flapping her arms around and her hair was bouncing up and down in the curls that she had let out of her curlers since I had seen her at the pool that morning. I couldn't understand what she was saying, but the one thing I could tell was that she was absolutely not happy.

Trevor was standing next to Bill's truck in the driveway, staring at Cindy with his mouth dropped open. His head was cocked to one side like when someone tries to talk to a dog and they look like they are trying their hardest to understand, but just can't quite make the connection. I supposed he would need an explanation of who in the world that woman was, so I made my way down to him.

"Who is that?" Trevor said when he realized I had dashed up next to him. Cindy's screeches continued on in the background.

"That would be Cindy Parker," I said, pointing towards her. "They call her the Poodle Lady or something like that. Her best friend was the one who was murdered this morning."

113

Trevor nodded, but turned back towards her with his mouth still dropped open in confusion. Cindy looked mad as a wet hen, stomping around her bicycle and waving her hands in the air. She was still yelling and every time she stomped, her extra tight, gray curls would bounce just enough to make her look like she was skipping around like a child.

A glance around told me that we had been the only ones dumb enough to actually emerge out into the open to watch this spectacle. There were an awful lot of cracked open windows and shades slightly peeked open, but everyone else had been smart enough not to let Cindy see them.

"Come on, I don't think anyone else is going to help her," I said. "But just know that Cindy isn't going to like you because Cindy doesn't like anyone. So just don't say anything to her. Let me talk to her."

Trevor nodded and together we walked down the street towards Cindy. As we got closer, I realized that the bicycle next to her couldn't possibly be her bike because unlike the falling-apart hunk of junk with a small hint of red, this bicycle was actually painted red and appeared to have been made in the past century. Confusingly, it still had her personalized license plate hanging off of it along with the basket though. It was almost like her bike had gone back in time.

"Cindy, what's wrong?" I asked as I got closer

to her. I tried to keep in mind that her best friend had just died this morning and that I needed to keep my sass in check. Cindy may be a woman who is hard to like, but everyone deserves to be treated with respect and care. "Is everything alright? Can I do anything to help you?"

Cindy stopped screaming and turned to look at us. She almost seemed like she was in a dream and immediately I recognized the dreamlike state of grief. After that moment of feeling for her, a vision of Mandy entered my head and I remembered that Cindy was also the reason Mandy was sitting at the police station right now.

"Someone has stolen my bike and replaced it with this one," she said, kicking the tire and making the bicycle tip over into a clanging, metal heap on the road. "I don't know who would do such a horrendous thing. They took my beloved bike and left me with this stupid thing."

"That looks like a pretty sweet bike actually," Trevor said from over my shoulder, ignoring the one piece of advice I had given him. I kicked him lightly in the shin, hoping he would remember that he wasn't supposed to be saying anything.

"Oh yes, this is a very sweet bike young man," Cindy said, her eyes narrowed at him before turning back to look at me. "The only logical explanation to this is that someone stole this bike from somewhere but when they almost got caught red-handed with it, they traded it for my old trusty bike."

So Cindy thought someone had stolen this bike, tried to take a shortcut through the RV park and switched it for Cindy's bike when they heard sirens? But somehow they took the time to give her back her license plate and basket before making the switch. That didn't sound like a logical explanation at all to me, but I got the feeling that Cindy and I operated on two very different wavelengths, so I didn't bother to point that out.

"I'd say you came out on top then," Trevor said, proving that not even a swift kick was enough to get hit to remember. "Someone took your bike and gave you a better one? I don't know what you have to complain about."

Cindy's scowl deepened even more. She looked Trevor over a bit before moving her gaze back to me.

"I suppose this idiot is with you?" she said. "He seems to match the intelligence level of you and your friend."

"Actually, I'm Mandy's boyfriend Trevor," he said, sticking out his hand towards Cindy.

Cindy stared at his hand like it might have an electric buzzer on it meant to give her a shock. Trevor's hand stayed out in midair like a beacon of optimism. I looked at his face, which had an expression of puppy-dog like happiness about it. Finally I reached over and pushed his arm back down by his side. Trevor took it in stride, simply smiling at Cindy with a small chuckle.

"So you're the boyfriend that won't propose?" Cindy scoffed. Seeing my shocked face, she continued. "I listen to the gossip around here. I might roll my eyes at it, but I listen. Boy, you seem to be a good relationship match with the killer of old ladies."

Trevor turned and looked at me. I felt like Cindy was practically spelling out her contempt for him, but his somewhat blank eyes covered by a sheet of hair he kept flipping over to the side were telling me he was still just not getting it.

"Trevor, Cindy is making fun of you," I said. "She is trying to get your goat. That is what she does. She drives around the RV park on her bicycle being cruel to people and trying to get them in trouble for small things that don't really matter so that she can get them kicked out of the park."

"Why would you do that?" Trevor asked, taking a step towards Cindy. "You must be a sad old lady."

Somehow Trevor's tone made it seem like he pitied Cindy. Now I was the one who was confused because I hadn't been able to muster up much sympathy for her, but somehow Trevor could. Maybe Trevor was a nicer person than the lazy, non-caring person I normally thought of him as.

"Takes one to know one," Cindy snapped.

I snorted before I was able to stifle my laughter. Cindy shot me a look, but I ignored it. I think she had finally met her match. Who knew her match would be the lazy man-child? No matter, I would still enjoy it.

"No matter what, we hope you figure out who took your hunk of junk and replaced it with a wonderful bicycle," I said. "It was very sweet of them to attach your basket and license plate for you. But Trevor and I really must be going because we are out on a walk."

I walked around the heap of tangled metal on the road and continued on towards the pool. When I noticed Trevor wasn't beside me, I turned around to see him picking up Cindy's stolen-but-not-by-her bicycle and balancing it on the kickstand before giving her a shy smile and dashing over to catch up with me.

Trevor may not be the best co-investigator, but he might just be an okay guy. I'd wait to make that judgment until later.

•Chapter Sixteen•

The gate to the pool area was open and while there was still police tape around the bushes on the outside, there wasn't any over the opening to the gate. I took that as a sign that I could go in and look around. Even if we were somehow caught in there, I could feign innocence. I felt a little twinge of guilt because Max would definitely chastise me for that line of thinking, but I would just leave that little bit of information out when I told him all about this later.

"Trevor, I need you to listen to me this time," I said, snapping my fingers in front of his face a few times. He shifted his gaze to me and I hoped that meant he was actually listening this time. "Technically I don't think we are supposed to be in there. But please take notice that there is no tape in front of the gate. And if we get caught by anyone in there, make sure we say we were totally oblivious to the fact that we weren't supposed to be in there. Does that make sense?"

Trevor shrugged his shoulders. I stared at him for a moment, wondering what that was supposed to mean. Trevor just stared back at me, so I took it to be an affirmative sort of shrug. I took a breath and walked through the opening.

I'm not sure what I expected, but the pool

looked exactly the same as it had the last two times I
had been in here except this time we were the only
people there and there was no obvious crime scene. It
looked like a very average sort of pool.

"How do people swim in that?" Trevor asked.
"It looks really small."

"They don't really swim, Trevor," I said. "You
have to remember that everyone who lives here is
retired. They just come down here and float around
on pool noodles. It's actually quite relaxing."

From the look on Trevor's face, I could tell that
the small pool was disappointing. He seemed like he
would be more of the sort to cannonball into the pool
rather than float around on a noodle. Oh well, it
wasn't like anyone was going to be swimming in
there for a while. Even once it wasn't a crime scene,
I'm sure they'd want it thoroughly cleaned after a
dead body floated around in it for a few hours.

I started to slowly walk around the pool,
looking all around. The police had already searched
down here and I'm sure they had found any clues
worth finding. I also knew that the police were still
unsure this was actually a murder so I had to hope
they didn't search as intently as they would if they
were certain of foul play.

Trevor was still standing where I had left him
by the gate. I took a deep breath to keep myself calm
before I shouted over to him.

"Hey, it would be helpful if you started looking around on the other side of the pool," I said, trying not to sound sarcastic. "If we each take half, we will be done and out of here faster."

The pool deck seemed very clean and I had to think that Bill kept it that way. He took his job as keeper of the pool seriously and everything look spotless. Well, I suppose it looked as spotless as an outdoor pool area could look.

Trevor had already reached the other end of the kidney shaped pool and he had plopped himself down on one of the pool chairs. He was leaned back like he was trying to get a suntan. I rolled my eyes, assuming I would still have to search the entire pool area despite having a helper who was turning out to not be much help.

A rustling in the bushes caught my attention and I started looking around frantically, wondering if it would look more suspicious to the police if I hid versus just standing out in the open as they came in. Either way, I would probably get in trouble. My stomach was twisting into knots as I tried to look casual.

Susie appeared in the opening for the gate, looking around furtively behind her. I breathed a sigh of relief that it wasn't the police but as she turned and caught sight of me, she jumped and let out a little yelp.

"What are you doing here?" she said.

She looked around and spotted Trevor in his reclined pose. He gave her a little smile and a wave. Susie raised her hand up and gave one unsure wave of her hand.

"I just wanted to come check out the pool area," I said gesturing around. "I wanted to show Trevor the pool."

Susie's eyebrows almost flew off her face and I suddenly remembered that no one knew Trevor because he had arrived during the hubbub that happened post-murder. So to Susie, all she saw was a guest of the park in the pool area crime scene with a strange, reclining man.

"Oh, that's just Trevor," I said. "He is Mandy's boyfriend and unfortunately he came down here to...umm surprise her by being here."

I had almost let out the big proposal surprise with my big mouth because I was so nervous. Susie just gave me an odd look and then shook her head. She seemed confused, still looking around the pool area nervously.

"Wait a second, why are you here?" I asked.

"Oh, I just thought it would be a good time to go for a swim," Susie said, holding up the towel draped over her arm that I hadn't noticed until just now. "Don't get me wrong, I love bobbing with the group. But I like to swim for exercise and I've never

122

been able to do it in the middle of the day. I thought this was the perfect chance."

Now it was my turn to give her an odd look. Had she forgotten that until just a few hours ago, there had been a dead body floating in the pool? I mean I guess I shouldn't judge and it looked like Hilda hadn't died in any sort of gruesome way, but still. I'm not sure I wanted to get back in that pool until it had been thoroughly cleaned.

"Don't you want to wait until they clean the stuff out from the dead body?" Trevor called from across the pool. I was glad he had said something because I wasn't sure how to respectfully phrase it, but Trevor cut right to the chase. There were a few advantages to his casual, breezy manner.

"Oh yeah, I didn't really think about that," Susie said.

She shifted from foot to foot and I wondered how she could seemingly forget about the death that had been the talk of the park all day today. Maybe she just really wanted to swim, but something was weird that I just couldn't put my finger on. Susie was fidgeting around like she was lying. Was she actually here trying to investigate like we were?

"Well, maybe swimming is a bad idea," she said. "I should maybe just head back home. You all should get out of here too. I'm pretty sure no one is supposed to be here. What exactly are you doing here anyways?"

Susie narrowed her eyebrows at me like she was focusing in on something. Maybe I should tell her the truth. She was one of the Dolls and I was pretty sure I could trust her to know that we were investigating.

"Okay fine, we are looking around for clues," I said. "Mandy didn't do this and we want to prove it. But don't tell anyone. We are kind of doing this in secret."

The heat of the day seemed to press in on us as Susie stared right at me. I wasn't sure what she was thinking but her eyes seemed to flash as she thought about what I said. She was still shifting around like she wasn't quite sure what to do.

"Oh I won't tell," Susie said finally, pressing her finger against her lips and winking at me. "It'll be our little secret. I will say there was someone else who had a confrontation with Hilda and Cindy last night. I don't want to point fingers, but Louise was awfully upset before I stepped in help her."

I had been so focused on Mandy's argument with the two ladies that I had almost forgotten that it had all started with Louise. I remembered Louise's determined face as she charged across the dance floor towards Cindy and Hilda. She had been wound so tight that she seemed almost ready for a physical showdown before Susie had stepped in.

"Do you really think Louise may have something to do with this?" I asked Susie.

She shrugged and threw her towel over her shoulder. It didn't seem likely to me, but Susie seemed pretty sure about it.

"All I'm saying is that she was very upset last night at Hilda and Cindy," Susie pointed out.

With one more shrug of her shoulders, Susie turned and walked out the pool gate. I watched the opening for a moment, almost hoping she would pop back in with more information but of course she was long gone. I turned to look at Trevor, who was still reclining on a pool chair. I couldn't see his eyes behind his sunglasses but I was pretty sure he had dozed off. He seemed to have the right idea even if it wasn't helpful at all.

It wouldn't really hurt if I took a little time to relax and think about the case. After all, I didn't want my investigative vision to be blurred by my fatigue and intense focus on finding other suspects. I sank down into one of the deck chairs, determined to kick up my feet and not move from that position for at least three minutes.

But as soon as I was relaxed in the chair, something caught my eye. Something was glinting in the sunlight from underneath a chair on the other side of the pool deck. I guess my three minutes of relaxation would be more like three seconds because I just had to know what was shining.

•Chapter Seventeen•

I walked around the pool, glancing over to see that Trevor was still asleep. By this point, I wasn't surprised. I thought about doing some mental soul-searching about my thoughts on Trevor and whether it reflected my undying, sisterly love for Mandy and the fact that no one would ever measure up to my incredibly high standards for someone to be worthy of her love. But right now, I needed to figure out what was glinting in the sun. It could be a clue or it could be a gum wrapper.

Hauling myself up from my reclined position on the deck chair, I swung my legs over the side and hoisted myself up. It wasn't so much my fatigue weighing me down as much as the fact that my once relaxing vacation was quickly draining away from me. I hadn't actually been on a vacation since Peter died and Mandy practically had to drag me onto the airplane even though I was excited for this warm weather vacation.

As I walked around the pool towards the reflection of light glaring towards me, I wondered why I didn't think I deserved a vacation like this. My life had changed so drastically that I don't think I felt like I deserved a vacation. I used to work at a high power, seventy-hour a week job that I poured everything into so that I could climb the corporate ladder. Peter had been doing the same thing and together, we were a career power couple. We worked hard but we also played hard. My old vacations seemed well-earned. After putting in hours and hours of overtime for weeks, Peter and I would jet off to some tropical destination where we spent three hours every morning answering emails before we put our computers away to relax for the rest of the day. I felt like I really earned those vacations.

But what did I do now that meant I needed a break? I hardly worked part time at the bed and breakfast where I lived with my parents. I volunteered my services to the city a lot like when I did marketing for the Halloween Hayride, but that didn't take much of my time either. Here I was, thirty years old and my life looked nothing like I thought it would. It didn't feel like I deserved this vacation I was on. Maybe that was why it was turning out to be more of a working vacation. Someone somewhere was having a good laugh at my expense.

By the time I was starting to really mire myself down in guilt, I had gotten around the pool to the chair that the reflection was coming from. I took a deep breath, hoping that whatever was underneath the chair wasn't just a piece of trash.

Bending down, I inhaled sharply and let out a loud yelp when I saw what it was, unable to keep my excitement inside. As I did a small victory dance to celebrate not being a total and complete loser at life, I noticed that Trevor had jumped to his feet at the sound of my shout. His sunglasses had slipped down off of his nose and were hanging over his mouth, his eyes wide over top of the rims.

"What, what?" he yelled as he scrambled to take his sunglasses off of his face. "Another dead body?"

I gave him a look. Unless I had found a murdered insect, how in the world would I have found another dead body that he couldn't plainly see? Part of Trevor's problem wasn't that he was dumb because he really wasn't. His problem was that he says whatever he thinks which means that he doesn't censor any of the stupid thoughts like the rest of us do.

"No, it isn't another dead body," I said, rolling my eyes at him. "But I did find something that may be a great clue. Come over here."

Trevor scurried around the pool but as he got closer, he stopped short and put his hands up. His mouth was puckered and his eyebrows were drawn together into an incredulous look.

"Wait, it isn't something that incriminates Mandy, right?" he said. "Because if it is, we should get rid of it."

"First of all, I am not investigating this in a way

that means I could potentially be locked up for hindering a police investigation," I said. Trevor looked at me like I was some sort of traitor. "If we found something that pointed towards Mandy, we wouldn't destroy it. We would just leave it but we maybe wouldn't tell the police we had found it."

"Isn't that kind of the same thing?" Trevor said.

"Umm it is and it isn't," I said, realizing that he was totally calling me out on my hypocrisy. "But second of all, do you really think I would be excited to find a clue that pointed to Mandy being the killer?"

Trevor shrugged his shoulders at me. I took a tissue out of my pocket and bent down, stopping before I picked up the metal object. I had known what it was the moment I saw it. By now I would be able to spot the official pin of the Dolls anywhere, especially because it said "The Dolls" right on it.

I was more interested on what was written underneath. The way it was sitting on the ground meant the reflection was obscuring the name that was engraved on the bottom of the pin.

"Sally told me that all of the Dolls have one of these," I said, pointing to the pin as Trevor knelt down beside me. "You can only have one if you are a member and they are all personalized. So when we pick it up, we will be able to see whose it is."

"But how do we know that it belongs to the murderer?" Trevor asked.

"Well, we don't," I admitted. "But I think we could narrow down how long it has been here depending on whose it is. The Dolls wear these pins to all of the social functions they attend in the park and tons of pictures were taken that night. We can check to see if they were all wearing their pins that night."

For a moment, Trevor and I both crouched together. We were in one of those moments of anticipation where I knew once we looked at the name, there would be no going back. It would set us on a path that we wouldn't be able to get off of. This clue could make or break our investigation.

Trevor nodded at me and I gingerly picked up the pin and held it on top of the tissue in the palm of my hand. I moved it so that it was in the shadow. As it moved out of the sun, the name at the bottom became clear.

LOUISE

I sucked in a large breath of air through my nose, half hoping I was reading the pin wrong and half trying not to let my mind race too much. Honestly, any of the names would have surprised me. I knew Louise wanted to fit in with the Dolls, but would she be willing to kill for that? Being a part of the Dolls didn't seem worth murdering poor Hilda, but I remembered Louise's desperate attempts to fit in with the more elegant ladies. She seemed willing to do almost anything to have the ladies like her more, even though she was already in the club.

"Trevor," I said. "I think it's time for you to meet Louise."

●Chapter Eighteen●

Louise's trailer wasn't hard to find because somehow it managed to resemble her. Where the other trailers were cutesy in an elegant sort of way with wicker deck furniture and beautiful cushions and pillows, Louise's trailer was trying too hard. Her furniture was over the top, painted wacky colors that didn't fit together. The cushions were all different patterns and while I know that pattern mixing can be quite chic, these patterns were just clashing.

Louise was sitting on a love seat with a little white dog on her lap. As we walked up the street and turned into her driveway, the dog stood up on Louise's legs and let out a small yip. The dog was wearing a little pink dress that was covered in rhinestones that shimmered in the sun.

"Eleanor, no bark," Louise said. "Hello there Tessa! Who is your friend?"

"Hi Louise," I said as we started up her deck stairs. "This is Trevor, Mandy's boyfriend."

Louise's face fell and she held her hands out to Trevor. Her hands were covered in big gaudy rings and while one or two of them probably had real stones, most of them appeared to be costume jewelry. Trevor stared at her hands for a moment before awkwardly bringing his hands up to hold them.

133

"I'm so sorry to hear about Mandy," Louise said, sniffing a few times. "She really is so sweet and I'm just sure she didn't do it."

Tears were forming in her eyes as she squeezed Trevor's hands. He winced in pain, but Louise didn't seem to notice. She started to loudly sob, her whole body shaking so much that the little dog on her lap bounced up and down, wildly shifting from side to side as she tried to keep her balance on Louise's leg.

"That's actually why we are here," I said. "Would this be a good place to talk?"

"No, no," she said. "Come on inside and we can have a little more privacy."

Following Louise through the door, the inside of her trailer was just as gaudy as the outside. There were trendy wall signs and knick-knacks everywhere along with overly dramatic curtains on every window. The couch had a loud, red and black plaid slipcover on it with some oversized cushions. Louise motioned for us to sit down on the couch. I wasn't sure if we were supposed to move the cushions or not when we sat down, so I just sort of scooted it to one side and squeezed between it and Trevor.

"Let me make us some tea," Louise bustling into the kitchen area.

"Do I really have to have tea?" Trevor asked quietly.

"Yes," I hissed at him. "But if things go the right

way, we won't be here long. I don't want to drag this out too much."

I sat and took a longer look around at Louise's living space. The kitchen had things hanging off of every cabinet knob but as Louise opened and closed them to get things out, somehow she managed to not slam any of them in the doors. The counter had bowls of fruit, canisters of baking supplies, a coffee maker, and all sorts of other things. While those were all totally normal things to have on a kitchen counter, an RV kitchen only has a very small amount of counter space. I wondered where she did any of the actual cooking.

In a way, the 'in-your-face' aspect of the RV made me feel a softening towards Louise. She could be loud and brash and, in your face, but I wondered if it was all just a cover like all of these things were a cover. Louise seemed like she desperately wanted to be liked but just wasn't sure how to make that happen.

"Here we go," Louise chirped as she set a tray of steaming teacups on a small TV tray in front of the couch. She shuffled back to the kitchen and came back holding her own teacup. She perched on a turquoise overstuffed chair that looked like it was too big to have been brought through the front door. I briefly wondered how they had managed to get the chair into the RV but then I remembered I had something much more important to focus on.

"Thank you so much Louise," I said. "You have a lovely place here."

"Oh geez, thank you Tessa," Louise said. "That's awfully nice of you to say."

"You know Louise, we were actually just out at the pool and we found something interesting," I said.

Louise was taking a sip of tea, but I could see her eyes widen over the rim of her teacup. Trevor wasn't even paying attention to what was going on. Instead, he was trying to figure out how to hold his steaming hot cup. He was holding the delicate handle between his thumb and forefinger while also trying to steady it with his other hand without burning his fingers. Once again, I could see that he was not going to be any help.

"Oh what were you out at the pool for?" Louise exclaimed. "If you wanted to show Trevor the sights, you probably didn't need to show him a place where someone died."

"Actually, we were there to investigate a little bit," I said. "See, I'm pretty sure Mandy did not do this and Trevor is also sure of that. So we decided to take matters into our own hands and poke around a little bit to see if we could help her out at all. And you know what? We found something pretty interesting there."

I reached into my pocket and pulled out what

136

ve had found. I slowly unwrapped the tissue from around the pin, being careful not to touch it. As the tissue fell away, Louise gasped and put her free hand over her face, her other hand still clutching the thin handle of her teacup.

"Obviously this is yours," I said.

Louise couldn't even look at the pin as she started to cry again. Trevor took advantage of Louise's distraction and set his teacup down on the tray. I almost elbowed him but as I went for the wind-up, a few drops of scalding hot tea spilled up and over the side of my teacup and burned my hand. I grudgingly put my cup down also, realizing that this wasn't the time for politeness anymore.

I looked back at Louise just in time to see the tea cup start to slip out of her hand. Leaping off of the couch, I stuck my hands out to grab the tea cup before it shattered on the ground. I managed to save the teacup, but only because I stuck my hands directly underneath all of the burning hot liquid that was falling out of the cup.

As I screamed, Trevor jumped to his feet and grabbed the teacup out of my hands. In one swift motion, he tossed it onto Louise's lap while he used his other hand to drag me back up to my feet. My mind was racing and I was trying not to focus on the pain that was shooting through my hands.

Trevor steered me into the kitchen and turned

on the faucet. Once he was sure the water was the right temperature, he forced my hands under it. The cool water flowed over my hands and I tried to take deep breaths through it.

After I was able to calm myself down a little, I could feel that while my hands definitely hurt and the burns would be annoying, it wasn't too terrible. If the tea was cool enough for Louise to be drinking, it wasn't hot enough to do any permanent damage.

Thinking of Louise, I turned to see what she was doing. To my horror, she was bending down to pick up her pin. When I leapt up to grab her teacup, I had dropped the pin on the ground. I wanted to go over and grab it from her, but Trevor was holding my wrists tightly, forcing my hands under the running water.

It was no use. Louise had already pinned it back on her shirt and now any evidence that may have been on it was ruined. I let out a cry as I realized how stupid the idea to confront Louise with her pin had been.

"It's okay Tessa," Trevor said quietly. "Your hands will be okay. We need to leave them under the water for another minute or so and then I'll drive you to the doctor to get them bandaged. They look okay though."

Trevor's quiet calm was so all encompassing that I immediately felt my heart rate go down a bit. I took a deep breath. Louise was sitting back in her chair, sipping her tea and absentmindedly petting Eleanor. At least she wasn't going to try to run away because I had already made one huge mistake and I didn't feel like making another.

•Chapter Nineteen•

Trevor kept glancing at his watch, timing how long my hands had been under the water. For someone I usually saw as a useless layabout, this must be the other side of him. This was the emergency dispatcher who kept calm and helped frantic people through some of the worst moments of their life. It did seem odd to me that these two people somehow inhabited one body, but maybe this was what Mandy could see in him that I couldn't.

At some point, Trevor let go of my wrists and turned the water off. My hands were red, but didn't look as bad as I thought they would. This was certainly not going to help my vacation, although that feeling of relaxation had gone out the window a while ago.

"Thank you, Trevor," I said. "I really appreciate it. I'm not sure what I would have done if you weren't here. But before we go, I'd like to just ask Louise one more thing."

Trevor nodded, doing the macho thing where he has a hard time accepting thanks. He took me by the elbow and guided me back to the couch where I sat back down. This time I didn't care about the cushions, sitting right on top of them.

Louise was still in her chair with Eleanor the

fluff ball, who was contentedly sleeping as her back was being scratched. Louise looked exactly as she had before our little medical interlude at the sink except now she was wearing the pin evidence. I wanted to kick myself for having dropped it.

"Louise, before we go to the doctor, I need to ask you how the pin got on the pool deck," I said. "Were you there when Hilda died?"

I wasn't going to mince words. I didn't have time to spend dancing around the point as I could feel the pain slowly coming back. The cool water had helped soothe them, but I needed to get to a doctor for some kind of cream and bandages soon. I glanced down at my red hands, glad the tea hadn't been any hotter or I may have been in serious trouble.

A loud cry broke the tension. Louise was sitting with her head thrown back, tears running down her face making black mascara paths. Her mouth was wide open in the sort of ugly cry that is uncomfortable to be an audience to, especially when it is coming from someone who is virtually a stranger.

I glanced at Trevor who glanced back at me with the same confused expression. Was this scene an admission of guilt? I didn't want to jump to conclusions since I had already made enough stupid mistakes today, but this was not the reaction of an innocent person in my mind.

The door of the camper flew open and Louise's

husband Roger came dashing in. He was dressed in a pair of khakis that had creases ironed into them and a button up shirt with a tie. It was a bit too formal, especially considering it was mid-afternoon and I was pretty sure he wasn't coming from any sort of job.

"Louise, what's wrong baby?" he said, looking back and forth from his sobbing wife to the two strangers sitting on his couch, one holding her beet red hands in the air.

The dog lifted her head and wagged her tail up and down a few times in greeting while Louise waved her hands around, fanning her face to dry the tears that had already ruined all of her eye makeup.

"Okay, I may as well tell all of you at once," Louise blubbered. "Roger, sit down honey."

Instead of finding a chair, Roger immediately plunked down on the floor where he had been standing. He crossed his legs like a kindergartner at story time, but his face was etched with worry.

"I was with Hilda at the pool last night," Louise said. "But I swear I didn't kill her."

Another sob escaped her mouth as the tears started trickling down her face again. Roger scooted himself forward enough that he could grab onto her hand and hold it. She looked at him with a pained expression. He squeezed her hand in response, making her smile a little.

"Why don't you back up and tell us from the

beginning," I said, trying to stay calm even though my hands were feeling more painful by the minute.

"Okay, so after the dance got all ruined last night, I wanted to find Cindy and Hilda to try to smooth over what had happened," Louise said.

She sniffled on and off as she talked. Trevor leaned forward and handed her a tissue that he had produced from somewhere. Louise grabbed the tissue and dabbed her cheeks with it, drying her tears and smearing the mascara.

"I just wanted to be the peacemaker because I thought that might help solidify my place in the Dolls," Louise said. " I always feel like I don't quite fit in and I've been doing everything I can to try to make sure they don't kick me out. I figure one way to cement my place was to fix this whole Cindy mess."

"But how did you end up with Hilda instead?" I asked.

"When I slipped out of the dance, I saw Hilda going into the pool area and I thought maybe Cindy was already in there," Louise said. "So I followed her in, but she was alone. I scared her even though I didn't mean to. Hilda said Cindy told her to come in and make notes about the fact that Bill hadn't done his job of closing up the pool for the night. She said Cindy was hoping to use it as part of her plan to get Bill and Sally kicked out of the park."

Louise let out another cry as Roger leaned over

and patted her leg. She put her hand lovingly on his face and gazed into his eyes. They both might have trouble fitting in, but they seemed to fit together perfectly.

"I tried not to get mad, but Hilda got all high and mighty about how she and Cindy were going to 'clean up the park' by kicking us all out," Louise said. "Hilda just wouldn't stop and she was smiling in such a smug way. And then I just snapped."

The air was all sucked out of the trailer as I hung on every word Louise said. I almost fell off of the couch with anticipation, biting my tongue to keep from spoiling the moment. Out of the corner of my eye, I could see Trevor's hands nervously clutching at the couch cushions.

"What happened between you and Hilda?" I asked quietly, trying not to prompt her too much.

"I pushed her," Louise said. "I put both arms up and I shoved her by the shoulders as hard as I could so that she fell backward. She tried to grab at me and that is when she must have hit my pin off of my shirt. Hilda fell right on her back and she hit her head on the pavement."

"And then she rolled into the pool?" I asked.

"No, at that point I ran away," Louise said. "I swear that when I left, Hilda was still just laying on the pool deck. I was so panicked at that point that I just needed to get away because I knew I could get in huge trouble for pushing her."

"How did Hilda end up in the pool then?" I asked. "Was she unconscious when you left?"

"No, she was totally with it, but she was mad as a wet chicken," Louise said. I could hear Trevor swallow back a laugh at Louise's language mistake. I almost elbowed him but neither Louise nor Roger seemed to notice it. Louise was taking some deep breaths while Roger held her hand.

"What did you do after that?" I prompted. Usually I tried to just let people talk, but my hands were starting to throb.

"Well, I was running towards home when Susie found me," Louise said. "She helped me the rest of the way home and asked if I was okay, but I couldn't possibly tell her what had just happened. The only thing I could say was that I had done something bad. Once I was all settled in, Roger came back home looking for me. I tossed and turned all night and then when I was puttering around making breakfast, I heard Sally scream up at the pool. That's when I went up there with Roger."

We all sat for a moment, letting the story hang in the air between us. Even if Louise didn't actually kill Hilda, Louise's story would probably help exonerate Mandy. I supposed the police could argue that Mandy came after Louise left and finished the job, but by that point Bill and Mandy were together.

Once again we were running into the same secretive roadblock.

"Louise, we have to tell the police," Roger said, firmly taking her by the hands.

A wave of relief washed over me. I wouldn't have to be the one to bring it up. Louise nodded slowly, taking another tissue that Trevor offered for her. She dabbed her cheeks and then loudly blew her nose.

"I'm going to take Tessa to the doctor," Trevor said, standing up from the couch. "Roger, I assume you will get Louise to the police station?"

Roger nodded, looking like a half-deflated balloon. It was obvious he loved Louise enough to see her through this ordeal. I just hoped that it would be enough for the police to release Mandy.

Trevor started tugging on my elbow, pulling me up to stand next to him. The pain in my hands was getting worse and worse. Hopefully a doctor visit wouldn't take too long so that it could coincide with picking Mandy up from the police station.

•Chapter Twenty•

An hour and a half later, Trevor and I walked out of the emergency room and back into the beautiful Florida day. I had two bandaged hands, a prescription for burn cream and most likely, a hefty bill that would arrive in my mailbox in a few weeks. What I didn't have was an answer to whether Mandy would be released or not.

Trevor's rental car was sitting all the way at the back of the very full parking lot and I had a brief feeling of gratitude that I wasn't on crutches or otherwise unable to walk the very long walk back there. The one nice bit was that after an overly air-conditioned stint inside the medical bay, the warmth of the sun felt amazing on my skin.

"Here you go, Tessa," Trevor said, holding the car door open for me.

I slid into the car, thinking about all of the nice things Trevor had been doing for me today. He walked around the car and got in, slipping a pair of sunglasses on. The car started with a roar and for just a moment I could see the appeal of a sports car.

"Trevor, can I just say a big thank you for all of your help?" I said. "You were so great helping me with my hands and getting me here to the doctor. Your investigation skills may be a bit sub-par, but your calm demeanor and medical knowledge really saved my day."

"No problem," Trevor said as he chuckled to himself. "I guess you are right about the investigating thing. I never would have gotten involved if Mandy wasn't the one who was being accused. I'm just glad I have you to do most of the legwork."

"At least I don't have to do the armwork," I said, refraining from making a rimshot sound effect afterwards.

Trevor just rolled his eyes at my lame joke and put his seatbelt on, helping me click mine in place. As we drove out of the parking lot, my cell phone started to ring. The little window on the outside of the phone said it was Bill calling but my bandaged hands made it almost impossible for me to open my flip phone so by the time I was actually able to answer it, the call had already been sent to voicemail. I quickly hit the button to redial.

"Tessa, are you there?" Bill said.

"Yes, yes, what's going on? Did Mandy get released?"

"Yes I did!" Mandy's voice came through the phone from somewhere in the background. "Come see me!"

"We will be right there," I said.

I shut my phone with a snap and turned towards Trevor. He stopped at a stop sign and turned o give me a puzzled look. I couldn't blame him for being cautious. He had planned everything out for a big surprise and it had all gone to pot.

"Drive to the police station," I yelled, throwing my bandaged hands in the air and waving them around. I know I looked like a weirdo, but I didn't care because I was so happy. "Cause we are picking up your girlfriend!"

We hooted and hollered until a car suddenly honked behind us. Apparently they did not share our enthusiasm for Mandy's release and only wanted to get wherever they were headed. Trevor hurriedly looked for traffic before making a turn and I shot a smile and a wave at the people behind us who had honked. Judging by their scowl, they did not forgive our extra-long traffic stop.

A few wrong turns later, we were pulling into the parking lot of a nondescript building that had the words POLICE DEPARTMENT above the front entrance. I could see Mandy and Bill sitting on a bench in front of the front doors with a man in a suit who, I deduced using my best investigative skills, must be the lawyer that Bill had called in.

"Hey, let's surprise her," I said before Trevor could actually park. "She still doesn't know you are here. Drop me off towards the back of the parking lot and then circle around to pick her up."

"That's a great idea," Trevor said, his dark eyes

glinting. "Get out here and I'll slowly circle until I see you are up there with them."

As soon as the car stopped at the back of one of the lanes of the parking lot, I practically fell out of the door because I was so excited to see Mandy. I ran down the middle of the parked cars waving aggressively towards Mandy as I yelled her name.

Mandy turned and smiled broadly at me, waving her hand just as excitedly as I was. A confused expression flew across her face as I remembered that my hands were heavily bandaged. After what seemed like way too much running, I was finally near the bench.

"I'm so excited you are out," I said. "So Louise's story must have worked, huh?"

"It sure did!" she exclaimed. "But what's with the mummy look? What in the world happened?"

I didn't think I should retell everything, so I gave an abridged version of the meeting at Louise's house and added in the clue that had brought us there along with Louise's story. By the end, Mandy was giggling and Bill had a wide smile on his face that I'm sure would be plastered there for a while. Only the strange man in the suit wasn't smiling.

"As admirable as your sense of duty and friendship are," the man said, "I'd appreciate for my client's sake if you would refrain from doing any more of this investigating that you think is helping.

I'm going to pretend I didn't hear about a potential clue that you gave back to a murder suspect."

I frowned at the sourpuss and hoped he was a super smart lawyer because his bedside manner could obviously use some work. But I trusted Bill's judgment. He must have seen something in this man to hire him.

"This is Mr. French," Mandy explained. "He's my lawyer. And the police did release me, but they told me I couldn't leave the area until they give me the go-ahead."

I stuck my hand out towards Mr. French, who gave a slight sneer before he reached out and grasped it. I gave it a vigorous shake. I wanted him on my side in case the police got upset at my investigation. Back in Shady Lake, I could count on Max to keep me out of jail as much as possible, but down here I didn't know any of the police officers.

"Hello Mr. French," I said. "My name is Tessa Schmidt and I am the reason your client was just released from police detention."

Mandy shot me a look that told me to cut the sass, but the twinkle in Bill's eye told me to keep it up. Before Mr. French could respond, I heard a car pull up and park behind me.

"Anybody need a ride?" Trevor said as he took off his sunglasses and got out of the car.

I looked straight at Mandy. Her eyebrows were

so high that they had almost become a part of her bangs and her mouth was wide open. She was so shocked she was completely frozen. Trevor came around the front of the car and waved at her at which point she finally moved, running to him and jumping into his open arms.

A glance at the large smile on Bill's face and I knew I was also grinning like an idiot. I tried to ignore Mr. French who was sitting on the bench watching us but seemingly unmoved by the entire situation. I wondered if this was his professional demeanor or if he was always a bundle of fun like this.

"That was great timing," Bill said, elbowing my arm. "You're such a great friend to Mandy. Thank you for everything you've done today."

We both turned and watched the happy couple, wrapped up in each other's arms and murmuring to each other. Mr. French finally stood up and with a promise from Bill to call if anything else happened, he returned to his fancy sports car and drove off.

Trevor opened the passenger door of the convertible and helped Mandy into the car before running around and hopping into the driver's seat. He revved the engine and with a small wave from both of them, they drove off into the sunset.

I leaned over to Bill as we watched the happy

couple drive away.

"You can give me a ride back to the RV park, right?" I asked.

•Chapter Twenty-One•

That night, I sat down to another dinner on the deck with Bill and Sally. I joyfully regaled them with every detail of my visit with Louise while they asked questions and laughed at all the funny parts. I also struggled to hold my fork with my hands all wrapped up, so I resorted to putting my grilled chicken on a bun and eating it as a sandwich instead.

"Tessa, I'm not sure we will ever be able to thank you for helping Mandy out so much," Sally said. "She would still be sitting in that police station if it weren't for you and Trevor. She may not be out of the woods yet, but it doesn't seem like she is the main suspect anymore."

I took another bite of my sandwich to make sure I didn't point out Trevor's very obvious lack of investigative skills. He still annoyed me a little bit but I had to admit that after spending time with him today he was growing on me, just a little.

With a wave of my hand, I dismissed the thanks. As a born and bred Minnesotan, I am always uncomfortable accepting thanks and with no one to deflect it to, I resorted to waving it into oblivion. In my mind, I had done what anyone would have done for their best friend.

"Speaking of Trevor, what do you think of

him?" Sally said. I looked at her and her blue eyes were locked on my face. She was searching for any emotion that my face dared to let slip.

"Oh he's good," I said, sipping from my wine glass. "Trevor's good."

"Out with it," Sally said. "Mandy has been very clear about the fact that you do not like Trevor. I have to say that as much as I know about him, I like him. But if he's here to propose, I'd like to hear from you exactly what you think of him so I know what to expect from my possible son-in-law. I want to know the good, bad, and the ugly."

The bite of sandwich in my mouth suddenly felt like I would need to chew it for an hour before I could swallow it. How should I answer that? My own feelings on Trevor were conflicted. Once upon a time, I had been convinced he was sort of a dirtbag who took advantage of Mandy. But since moving back to Shady Lake and actually spending a little time with him, I was seeing things I never would have thought would be there.

I kept chewing even though the bite had practically disintegrated in my mouth. After I swallowed, I picked up my wineglass and took a sip. Over the bubbly white wine, I could see Sally's eyes trained on me. She was not going to let me off easy with this one. Bill was more focused on his dinner and on the fact that he had a poker game to attend in about five minutes. I decided to go for the compliment sandwich, which I had once learned about as a nice way to critique someone. While telling someone about something negative, it helps to make sure it is surrounded by positive things.

"Well, it is obvious that Trevor loves Mandy a lot," I said, using the obvious as a jumping off point before moving on to the not so nice point. "I do think he could work a little bit on his lackadaisical attitude towards life in general."

"Mmm hmm," Sally said. Her elbows were on the table and her hands were folded together with her chin propped on top of them. I got the feeling that Sally would have made it very far up the corporate ladder if she hadn't been so busy running a donut shop.

"But I think he is working on being a bit more mature than he has been," I said, ending with another statement that was about as much of a compliment as I could get for Trevor.

Bill stood up, seemingly oblivious to our conversation but sat back down when Sally gave a wave of her hand.

"I'm going to put you on the spot here Tessa," she said. "After Bill and I, you are the person who is the most concerned with Mandy's well-being. Would you want her to marry Trevor?"

"Yes," I said immediately. "Yes she should

marry Trevor."

For once, I shot off my big mouth and used it for good instead of just using it to get in trouble. Actually, the answer just tumbled right out of my mouth and surprised everyone, most of all me. Sally gave a little smile before nodding at Bill. He took that as a sign that he could now leave for his card game and he took the out, practically skipping down the stairs and out of sight down the street.

"Here I thought you would say no," Sally said. She sat back in her chair, casually holding her wine glass in one hand. "I don't want to throw Mandy under the bus, but she has frequently complained to me that you didn't like Trevor and she wasn't sure how to balance both of you."

I let out a big exhale. Man, sometimes I was a lousy friend. A few tears started to sting my eyes and I blinked a few times, hoping to push them back. This trip was bringing up all sorts of emotions.

"I'm not sure what to say," I said.

I picked up my wine glass and glanced away, taking a small sip and hoping that Sally wouldn't see me cry. A tear spilled over and I felt it run down my cheek. A brief vision of Louise's mascara streaked face flashed in my mind and I wondered how she was doing. Was she telling the truth when she said she hadn't actually killed Hilda, just pushed her down? If anyone could get the answers, I suppose the police could.

"Tessa, I didn't mean to upset you," Sally said quietly. "But I value your opinion of Trevor because after Bill and I, you know Mandy the best and you are watching out for her. Trevor has his downsides, but we only get the positives from Mandy. I wanted to know what you honestly thought so I had a good idea what Mandy was getting herself into. They've been together a long time, but that doesn't always mean people should get married."

"I don't think I'm crying because of what you said. I'm crying more because I'm realizing that Mandy deserves a much better friend than me. She's been with Trevor for a decade and I can't even be supportive and happy for her? But spending a little time with Trevor has changed that, especially since he has started to try and mature a bit lately."

Sally stood up and walked over to my chair. She knelt down beside me and put her thin, cool hand on my cheek. As more tears dripped down, she used her thumb to wipe them away. It was the kind of gesture that was so intimate that I instantly felt closer to Sally. All of my guilt melted away as I felt the love between us. Sally used to be like my second mother and even though I had been a bit of a prodigal son, she was still willing to love me.

I turned and gave Sally a hug, who hugged me back. She scooted herself back into her chair and smiled at me. A sense of calm slid over me and for the first time during this entire vacation, I felt comfortable around Sally. I finally felt the acceptance I knew she had been offering the entire time.

Sally stood up and flitted into the sun room, emerging with a tray of cookies. I picked one up and started to take a bite, but before I could enjoy my dessert after a hard day's work, a voice broke through the evening air.

"So, you really want Louise to be put away for murder, huh?"

I froze as the guilt seemed to rain down and I turned to face my accuser.

•Chapter Twenty-Two•

Susie was parking her sleek and shiny racing bike next to the truck in the driveway. She kicked out the kickstand and took extra care to balance the bicycle in the gravel driveway, making sure it didn't wobble at all before she came up the stairs towards us. It was quite the contrast to Cindy pushing over her nice bike into a heap this morning.

"Roger just got a hold of me and told me that you practically forced Louise to go into the police station to tell them about the accident," Susie said.

She took off her helmet and ran her fingers through her short gray hair. It stuck up in all directions but instead of looking crazy, somehow it matched her sporty style. As I struggled to come up with something to say, Susie continued on.

"I just think it was a crazy accident," Susie said with a shrug. "If Mandy didn't do it and Louise says Hilda was fine when she left the pool area, I think everyone should just leave well enough alone. Let's not ruin everyone's lives over a puzzle like this. Hilda should be remembered for who she was, not for how she died."

"I agree with you on that," Sally said. "But I think if the police are still suspecting murder, it should be investigated and someone should be held

160

accountable."

"Someone should be held accountable," Susie said. "And it's that horrible Cindy for getting us all in this mess."

"I'm not sure that's the right way to think," Sally said as she pointed to one of the open chairs on the deck.

Susie hesitated for a moment before she strode over and decisively sat down, her back ramrod straight. She may be willing to sit down, but she was not going to relax for one second. There was an energy coming from her that I couldn't quite figure out. She seemed upset about Louise, but there was something else there that was complicating everything.

"Susie, you were the one who pointed us towards Louise," I said, pushing the tray of cookies her way. I thought that if I could get her to eat a cookie, maybe she would relax a little bit. "When we bumped into you at the pool, you suggested we pay her a visit."

"You're right," she admitted. "But apparently I shouldn't have done that. I thought she was innocent and I figured she would tell you what she had been up to the night of Hilda's murder. When I walked her home that night, she was very upset. She wouldn't tell me why but I just figured that her feelings had been hurt."

"Why would her feelings have been hurt?" Sally asked, tipping her head to one side.

She was cool as a cucumber and I could see why she was the Queen Bee of the Dolls. As always, Sally was impeccably dressed in a sundress with sandals that laced up her legs. She somehow managed to balance style with dressing for her age in a way that I marveled at and thought maybe I should take notes on to remember once I was older.

Right now, Sally sat back in her chair and quietly waited for Susie to talk. She had a cookie on a plate in front of her that had exactly one bite taken out of it. I had the feeling that the secret to her healthy physique was eating delicious foods, but taking time to savor them. I made a mental note of that also.

Susie, on the other hand, was sitting on the edge of her chair with her hands on her knees. She looked so uncomfortable that I almost stood up to get her a pillow for her back but I didn't want to break the spell that Sally seemed to be putting her under.

"I may have said some harsh things to her after the fight with Cindy at the dance," Susie said.

"You may have?" Sally asked, one eyebrow arched.

"Okay, I did," Susie mumbled. She stared at her hands as if they might run away if she didn't keep an eye on them. "I told her that if she wanted to keep her place in the Dolls, she should sit down and shut up. I told her that if she kept up with those kind of shenanigans, that we may have to replace her."

Sally exhaled as she shook her head. Susie glanced at Sally and immediately put her head back down, reminding me of a puppy who is being scolded. I knew the sort of expression on Sally's face was one of those 'I'm not mad, just disappointed' faces that parents become so good at making.

"Susie, we never replace a Doll," Sally said. "Once they are in, they are a Doll for life."

"Well I know that, but Louise didn't know that," Susie said, sounding a bit flustered. "I was just trying to be helpful."

Susie's cheeks were slowly getting red. Sally stayed silent for a while as we all thought about what Susie had said. Susie was looking around, trying to avoid Sally's hard stare. It was obvious Susie knew how terrible it sounded and she knew she had made a big mistake.

"I think you should go home, Susie," Sally said. "Go home and think about things a little bit. I need some time to figure out how to handle this situation."

Susie stood up and jammed her bicycle helmet back on her head. She walked down the stairs but as soon as she neared her bicycle, she whipped back around. Her eyes were zeroing in on me.

"Oh, there was one more thing," she said. "I was here to invite Tessa on the bicycle outing with the

Bike Brigade the day after tomorrow."

I looked at her quizzically. Why would she come to invite me on a bicycle outing? Susie's eyes darted around. I glanced at Sally, who looked just as confused as I was.

"I thought I heard someone say that Tessa loved to ride bikes," Susie said with a shrug of her shoulders. "I thought the polite thing to do would be to ask her to the little bike ride with the club. You don't have to if you don't want to."

For someone who had charged up here on her bicycle slinging anger at me, she seemed exceptionally hurt that I wasn't immediately jumping at the chance to join the Bike Brigade for a ride.

"That would be fun Susie," I said. "But I don't have a bike or anything, so even if I wanted to go with you, I wouldn't be able to."

"Oh I can take care of that," Susie said with a wave of her hand. "I have a few extra bicycles and helmets. Why don't you stop by tomorrow morning to pick them up so that you can make sure the helmet fits and you have a whole day to get used to the bicycle before we go."

Before I could respond, Susie climbed on her bike and pushed off. She waved as she rode down the street into the sunset.

"See you tomorrow morning," she called before turning the corner and riding out of sight.

Sally and I both took a much needed drink from our wine before I turned to her. She still looked just as puzzled as she had when Susie had invited me on the bike ride.

"Did you tell her that I liked to ride bicycles?" I asked.

"No, I have no idea what your thoughts are on bicycles," Sally said. "I wouldn't have told her that. Maybe she confused you with someone else's guest? The only thing I told her was about how you like to investigate things and you are interested in true crime. Usually she's pretty sharp though so I'm surprised she got it mixed up."

"Are you able to come riding with me?" I asked. For some reason, I just really didn't want to go on this bike ride alone.

"I'm sorry honey, but we double booked activities that day," Sally said. "I am running bingo."

I poured us each one more glass of wine and we watched the sunset together while we waited for Bill or the two lovebirds to get back home. I also steeled myself for the bike ride I was now emotionally obligated to go on. It could go one of two ways: either the club would be mostly regular old people who just wanted a fun, leisurely bike ride or it would be the kind of vigorous exercise that kept Susie in shape.

My hope was that it was the first kind of ride

because I may not survive the second.

•Chapter Twenty-Three•

After Bill came home and he and Sally went inside to watch the nightly news, I pulled out my phone to call Max while I tried to wait for Trevor and Mandy to come back. I just had to see if Mandy would come back with a diamond ring. I had no idea when Trevor was going to propose now that his plan had been ruined so it was going to be a surprise for everyone.

As soon as Max answered his phone, I felt my body melt back into the chair. His deep voice was so calming that I couldn't help but feel even more in love with him. I shut my eyes, picturing his smiling face in my mind, wishing he was here with me.

"I'm so glad you called Tessa," he said. "I've missed you so much but I don't want to bother you while you are on your relaxing vacation."

I snorted at the thought of relaxing on this vacation. Until that very moment, I don't think I really had time to relax. My time had been filled with a nerve-wracking plane ride, a full schedule of events to schlep around to and then a murder investigation. It sounds more like a nightmare than anything else.

"You are never a bother to me," I said. "I miss you too. I can't wait to come back and see you."

"I can't wait to see you either Sweet Thing,"

Max said. "Maybe I can come up Friday and get you from the airport. You will still be able to come home Friday, right?"

Max's voice clouded a bit, his concern for my well-being pinging straight through the satellite and down into my phone. He knew that if Mandy had to stay down here, there was no way I would leave Florida without her. I brought him up to speed on everything that had happened today, mostly about Louise's story and Mandy getting released. The one thing I conveniently left out was my stupid thought that I could catch a teacup and the burning hot contents spilling out of it. I hoped that by the time I saw him again, my hands would be mostly healed and I could spin it as more of a funny story.

"The only thing is that Mandy is supposed to stay close until they get everything figured out," I said. "So I'm a little worried because Louise swears that Hilda was still very much alive when she left the pool area. The confession I got was only part of a confession."

"Do you think that is because Louise is lying or do you think that is because she really didn't kill Hilda?" Max asked.

That was a great question that I had not put any thought into yet. I had been more focused on piecing together the story and not so much on my feelings about it. I picked up my glass of water and took a good long drink. My vacation self kind of wished it was more wine, but my practical self knew I needed to stay hydrated if I wanted to feel good tomorrow.

"I need to think about that a little more," I said. My head was a bit clouded by the wine from earlier and I didn't want to jump to one conclusion or the other without some thought. I shelved the question to mull over later. "But I didn't call for more investigation help. I've been doing enough investigating today because I have to do all of my investigating and all of Trevor's too."

Max laughed a gut laugh. The chuckle felt like home and suddenly I felt such a magnetic pull towards Max. Sometimes I wondered if dating Max was just a safeguard I put in place. Like maybe I fell back into this relationship because I needed comfort and not because I actually needed Max. I worried that my broken self would one day be mended and I would discover that I wanted to move on. Whether or not I loved Max romantically, I would never want to hurt him.

But in that moment, sitting in the warmth of a Florida evening under a strand of lights on the deck, talking to Max filled me with such a sense of warmth and comfort and love. This man had saved me from killers and he had saved me from myself. I felt like I was looking into a pool of the love I felt for him and it was so deep, I couldn't even begin to sense a bottom. For what seemed like the first time, I was certain that my love was totally and genuinely true.

"Max, I love you," I blurted out, interrupting his laugh. "I know I say that a lot, but I really want you to know that deep down, I love you."

"Where did that come from?" he asked, his voice tender. "And I love you too, more than you'll ever realize."

"I've just been thinking about our relationship and where we are going," I said. "I wanted to make sure that what we had seemed real. I guess what I want is to make sure that we are traveling this path with some sort of destination in mind, some kind of future together."

When Max and I had started our relationship, we had been very clear that we were just being casual. We were so casual that we weren't even exclusive. It had been less than a year since both of our spouses had died and we were just dipping our toes into the dating world again.

But now I could separate my grief over Peter's death from my love of Max. It didn't feel like I was trying to use Max to replace Peter. It felt like Max had revitalized this new chapter of my life. I felt like I had fully turned to the next page.

"Tessa, I want you to know that I want us to be together now and in the future," he said. "I want us to be together forever. I'm not sure we need to make a concrete plan right here and right now but if you want me to say it, I'd like to marry you someday."

My heart exploded into a million pieces and butterflies erupted in my stomach. I couldn't help but giggle a little as I replayed Max's words in my head.

"I want to be your wife someday," I said. "And no, we don't have to start setting dates or anything. But just hearing you say that makes me so sure that we are doing the right thing. I'm just so happy with you."

"My biggest goal in life right now is to make you happy," Max said. "Making you happy makes me happy. And we have both been through too much sadness in our lives. We deserve this happiness."

I smiled. When someone looked at Max, he looked exactly how a police officer should look. He was stocky and muscular with a stern face that could crack a smile in an instant. He had an air of authority but also one of fun. Deep down inside, he was also full of love and kindness.

"I should let you go," I said. "You need to work tomorrow and I'm hoping to see Mandy and Trevor before I go to bed. I'm not sure when he is going to propose and I want to be the first one to know."

"Okay Sweet Thing," Max said. "Just don't stay up too late. I love you more than words can say."

"I love you too Max," I said.

We hung up and I tilted my head back and watched the stars above me. It was a bit cliche to think about how the stars I was looking at would be the same stars Max may glance at on his way to bed, but I couldn't help it. I was simply bursting with romance and hearts and sweet thoughts.

•Chapter Twenty-Four•

Mandy didn't get home until almost midnight and by then I had retired to the pull-out sofa, but I wasn't actually asleep. There was no big to-do and no ring on her finger, so I didn't ask about the proposal. In fact I was so tired by that point that I didn't even tell her about the strange bike ride I was now obligated to take.

After a breakfast where I tried to explain the mysterious bike ride and Mandy absolutely refusing to accompany me on it, I left to go over to Susie's trailer to try out some bikes. Sally gave me directions, but it wasn't hard to find as she only lived two trailers down from Sally and Bill.

It was one of those delicious mornings where I had to slip a sweatshirt over my t-shirt and shorts, but I could feel that it would be warming up to be another amazing day. As much as I loved Minnesota with my whole heart and wouldn't dream of living somewhere that didn't have four seasons, I could see the appeal of Florida and why it attracted so many Minnesotans.

Susie's driveway looked like a bicycle parking lot, if there were such a thing. There was a very small electric car and then six bicycles that all fit in their driveway and glancing at all of them, none was as pretty as the one I'd seen Susie riding the other day.

In fact, most of them looked more like Cindy's old bike and I briefly wondered if that hunk of junk had ended up here. But none of them looked as junky as the one Cindy used to have.

I glanced around, wondering if I was supposed to knock on the door of the trailer. It was still pretty early and I didn't want to wake her up if she was still sleeping.

"Hey there," a voice came from behind me.

I turned around to see Susie and her husband riding up behind me on their sleek, sporty bikes. They were both decked out in all spandex with the sort of aerodynamic bike helmets that are only spotted on serious riders. I wondered if that meant tomorrow's ride would be a bit more aggressive than I had hoped.

"Oh hi, I'm glad you're awake," I said. "When I came and didn't see you, I was afraid I would wake you up if I knocked on the door."

Susie and her husband both laughed. They parked their bikes and took off their helmets to reveal matching short, gray haircuts.

"Oh we get up with the sun every day to get our miles in," Susie said. "Why don't I help you find a bike and helmet?"

Susie's husband was a man of few words, simply giving me a wave as he went inside the trailer. Susie, on the other hand, was already blathering on about all of the bicycles and what their differences

174

were. Honestly I didn't really care because to me, a bicycle was a bicycle was a bicycle. I just needed something to ride if I was being forced to join in on this ride.

"I think this bicycle is probably the best one for you to ride," Susie said, wheeling a rusty green bicycle forward. She seemed almost jittery as she talked. "I also have a helmet you can borrow. Let me go grab that and then you'll have time to practice riding the bike before the ride tomorrow."

Susie scuttled off to the trailer while I walked around the bicycle. I hadn't been on a bicycle in over a decade, but considering the old saying, I really hoped I could just get on and ride without much trouble.

"Here we go," Susie said, slamming the door of the trailer open as she waved a bike helmet at me. "Try it on so we know it fits just right."

I put the blue helmet on my head and buckled it under my chin. I struggled to tighten the straps, but Susie stepped up and tightened it for me. It was a bit awkward to have someone I hardly knew doing something that felt so weirdly intimate. She was so close to my face that I was immediately self-conscious. I held my breath, hoping it wasn't smelly.

Once the helmet was adjusted, I wondered if it would be rude to just leave. I don't know what was wrong with Susie, but she seemed nervous and being this close to her was making me feel nervous. I didn't need any more nerves; going for this bike ride with the Brigade would be enough.

"I should probably go," I said. I grabbed the handlebars and started to wheel the bike down the driveway before Susie called after me.

"How is your investigation is going?" Susie called. "Have you solved the murder yet?"

So she did remember what Sally had said about me. Why did she invite me on the bike ride then? Out of all of the Dolls, I think Susie was becoming the one I was the least comfortable with. First, she had been intimidating with how physically fit she was for her age, but now she seemed so jumpy that I felt like I had butterflies in my stomach too.

"No, I haven't solved it although Mandy has been released," I said. "That was what I was most concerned about."

"Yeah, that makes sense," Susie said. "Say, did you ever find Louise's pin at the pool?"

I waited for a moment before turning around. I didn't think I had said anything about Louise's pin and not many people knew about it. Maybe she had heard that from somewhere else. I shrugged it off, thinking Louise must have gotten in touch with Susie to let her know since she had been the one looking for the pin.

"Yes we did," I said cautiously. "How did you know about Louise's pin?"

Susie nervously twitched a little, rubbing her hands together as she chuckled a little. She touched her pin a few times, rubbing it a little like she was polishing it.

"Well remember I said that I found Louise that night and walked her home," Susie said. "When we got there, I noticed that the pin was gone and so I went looking for it once Roger came back to care for her."

"So you went back to the pool that night?" I asked. I was trying to dance around what I meant, but Susie seemed to understand what I was gunning for. She immediately put her hands up, backpedaling from what she said.

"No, no, no," she said. " I just went looking for the pin, I never said I went to the pool."

"Where did you look then?" I asked.

The night of the murder, we had looked all over the park for Louise and Susie and come to think of it, we never really did find Susie. Apparently she was looking for this pin somewhere. Wouldn't we have stumbled upon her at some point if she was really looking all over for Louise's pin?

"I looked in the gymnasium and on the patio," she said.

Susie blinked at me and I stared right back. The way she was acting made me think she was lying, but I couldn't really call her on anything. I didn't know the truth and I knew that she wasn't going to tell me.

"Okay, it sounds like you looked really hard," I said, feeling a bit lame but it was the only thing I could think to say. "But we did find the pin. I should probably go though. I'd like a little time to practice riding the bike."

"Yeah, you should ride a little bit," Susie, a piercing stare cutting through me. "We wouldn't want you to have some sort of accident today and be unable to finish up your investigation."

I chuckled uncomfortably. It seemed like such a menacing statement even though Susie had followed it up with a little smile. I wasn't getting good vibes from Susie, so I decided I needed to get out of there right away. I gave a little wave and walked the bicycle down the driveway to the street.

"I was just making a bad joke," Susie called after me. "I'm just concerned about Louise, that's all."

I turned and gave another little wave with a smile. Something was telling me that I wanted to stay on Susie's good side. She wasn't telling me the whole truth, but I also wasn't sure what she was lying about. Once I was out of Susie's view, I got on the bike and tried to focus on keeping my balance.

It looked like maybe riding a bike wasn't

something I could just pick up and do again after so many years. Good thing I had some time to practice.

•Chapter Twenty-Five•

After a few spins up and down the streets of the RV park, I was feeling much more comfortable with my skills, even if bike riding did seem to take all of my concentration. I didn't want to waste all of my sort of beginner's luck on riding around the RV park so I steered my bicycle back towards home.

When I got to Bill and Sally's RV, there was a golf cart parked next to the truck that I didn't recognize. I could see Bill and Sally sitting with someone inside of the screened-in sun room, but it didn't look like Trevor or Mandy. I kicked the kickstand down and took off the bike helmet before I went to see who they were meeting with.

Bill and Sally sat together on a little loveseat while a pudgy, balding man sat on a chair across a table from them. Everyone seemed smiley and happy, so I had to assume this wasn't related to the murder.

"Oh hi, Tessa, I'm so glad you're back," Sally said as she gestured for me to sit in the chair next to the rotund man. "I wanted to introduce you to Tom. This is Tom Parks, the owner of the park. He came by to talk to us about Cindy."

"Again," Bill muttered under his breath.

Tom held out a pudgy hand for me to shake and as I grasped it, he shot me a big, friendly smile.

From all I'd heard about Tom, he was on the side of the Dolls, if there were any sides in all of these shenanigans. I let go of his hand and sat down.

"It's nice to meet you Tessa," Tom said. "I'm glad you're visiting the park, but I'm sorry it's been a bit more exciting than our little retirement park usually is. Although from what I hear, you enjoy investigating these sorts of things."

If someone would have told me a few years ago while I was still living in a high rise apartment and working a corporate job that I would someday be known for my love of true crime and solving gruesome puzzles instead of anything else, I would have thought that person was off their rocker. But here I was trying to piece together clues to figure out how an elderly lady died.

"I think you're right about the excitement," I said with a chuckle. "It has certainly livened things up here. But Sally said you were here about Cindy. What is that all about?"

Tom let out a big exhale, comically puffing out his cheeks to show that he didn't like being in the middle of all this. But as the owner of the park, it was just the sort of dispute that he had to deal with.

"Hoo boy, well it is about what it is always about," Tom said. "Cindy wrote me an email the night of the murder with more accusations about Bill and Sally, saying that she wanted them kicked out and she had friends that would help make that happen and yada, yada, yada. The first thing she wanted was to have Bill removed as the Keeper of the Pool, which is a no-go because I had absolutely nothing to do with that and the Dolls were the ones who appointed him unofficially. I told her she would have to take it up with Sally and the ladies."

"And I'm assuming she didn't take that well?" I asked.

Bill rolled his eyes as Sally gave him a playful shove before she got up and headed over to the bar area. Tom grimaced and put his meaty hands out as he struggled to find the words he wanted.

"Look, Cindy is a real character," Tom finally said. "She isn't easy to get along with and she isn't the sort of fun person that this RV park normally attracts. But Cindy hasn't done anything wrong, even if she is annoying. I try my hardest to balance her concerns with the wellbeing of everyone else in the community. I address anything that may be valid and ignore the rest."

Sally came back with a tray of lemonade and some muffins. I poured myself a drink and chose a blueberry muffin, hoping the fruit inside meant it was just the tiniest bit healthier for me than the chocolate chip ones, not that it should matter too much since I was on vacation after all.

"But Tom, before Tessa came in you said you

needed to tell us something important," Bill said, taking the wrapper off of his muffin. "Was it just about the emails?"

"Well no, there was something else," Tom said. "The police asked if I had any security tapes I could bring in that they could use as evidence. I told them that I would bring everything from the night of the murder but we don't actually have a camera that would have captured the murder. The closest we have is one that faces the pool area of the big patio, but the hedges block the view of anything actually happening around the pool."

Tom took a big gulp of lemonade, his eyes darting around as he did everything he could to avoid eye contact with us. He nervously scratched his forehead and cleared his throat a few times.

"I'll just come out and say it," he said. "As I was watching the tapes this morning, I found one of Mandy stealing Cindy's bike and causing some pretty significant damage to it. Bill, it shows you too."

Bill deflated, his head hanging low as Sally narrowed her eyes at him. Her mouth was set in a concerned pucker as she reached over and put her hand on his shoulder, showing him that she would stand by him, but she wasn't happy about what had happened.

So Mandy had been the one to take Cindy's bike. Mandy wasn't normally one to have a temper, but her protective instincts seemed to have come out that night at the dance.

"After Mandy left the dance that night, I went out to find her," Bill said. "By the time I came across her, she had already smashed up Cindy's bike pretty bad. It was in rough enough shape before, but I knew at that point that there was no way I could fix it up. So we took Cindy's personal things off of it and tossed the bike in the dumpster and then she and I headed out to find a bike to buy."

"But you guys were gone most of the night," I said. "Where in the world did you go?"

"There aren't many bicycle shops that are open twenty-four hours a day," Bill said. "So we ended up at one of those big box stores where we managed to buy a red bicycle that we hoped would make her happy."

"So Mandy didn't kill someone in a fit of rage, but she did destroy a bicycle," Sally said slowly, trying to understand all of the pertinent details in this strange new story.

"Yes, but once she stopped and thought about it, she realized that Cindy would definitely turn her into the police for destroying her property," Bill said. "We hoped that we could stop all of that by buying her a new bike, but of course she doesn't seem to be happy with that either."

"I just wanted to warn you because I did have

o turn the tape into the police, but I thought you should know when they come to ask questions," Tom said.

"Thank you, Tom," Sally said. "I do appreciate it."

"I really should be going," Tom said. "There are always lots of things to do around here, mostly checking in on the supposed violations I am alerted to each week."

With a wink, he slipped out the door. We all sat in silence for a moment, listening to the beep of Tom's golf cart as he backed it out of the driveway. The lemonade Sally had brought over was the perfect mix of sweet and sour and I took another sip.

Mandy was usually the calm, even-keeled one while I was the brash one who did and said things without thinking. I was getting a glimpse into her world, which apparently involved a fair amount of figuring out how to help me get out of a jam.

Cindy had probably already reported her stolen bike to the police along with the "dumping" of a brand new bike on her front porch. When the police looked at the security tapes, they would clearly see Mandy destroying the bike so I had to assume they would come to get her again. I'm not sure there was much I could do, although at least I was pretty sure Mandy could get off with a just a fine for this.

"Let's look at the bright side, I'm sure there

won't be any jail time looming over Mandy for this," I said.

"There will be if Cindy has any say in it," Bill said with a snort. "She'd probably demand life in prison for daring to replace her ancient, hunk of junk bicycle."

We all laughed, imagining Cindy in court trying to haggle with the judge for a life sentence. In my mind, her overly tight, curled hair was bouncing up and down as she stomped on the ground demanding justice. That image of her was sadly not that out of the norm for Cindy.

"Oh Bill, be nice," Sally said once she stopped laughing. "We shouldn't judge if Cindy loved her bicycle. For all we know, it was a treasured heirloom."

"It definitely was not," Bill said. "I know that because she bragged to me once that she found it leaning against a trash can on garbage day. Cindy was pretty proud of finding a working bicycle for free."

After we finished our snack of lemonade and muffins, I thought about what Tom had said. He had handed all sorts of security tapes over to the police. I wondered if he would let me watch them also. It was worth a shot, so I clicked my helmet on my head and hopped on my bicycle to go have a chat with Tom.

•Chapter Twenty-Six•

Riding through the park was actually kind of fun now that I had my bicycle legs under me. The more I rode, the more comfortable I felt and the less I had to concentrate on the actual riding of the bike. It was a bit like being back in Shady Lake because everyone I passed by waved and called out a greeting to me. Some of them I recognized, but others were completely unfamiliar but still very nice.

Tom's office was a tiny little building next to the entrance to the RV park that looked like a garden shed. In fact the more I looked at it, the more it looked like it had been purchased at a home improvement store and plopped here unceremoniously. There was a little hand-painted sign above the door that said TOMS OFFICE. I cringed a bit at the lack of apostrophe, but soldiered on.

I knocked a few times on the door before I tried the door handle. It was locked, but then I noticed a tiny sign stuck above the doorknob. It was so small and in such an odd place that I was a bit surprised I had noticed it at all.

Out for lunch it read. *Be back in an hour or so.*

I'd just have to wait to see those tapes. Thankfully the ride with the Bike Brigade wasn't until tomorrow, so I had all afternoon free to check back in with Tom. I was about to get back on my bicycle when I could hear a bike ride up behind me.

"Hey, what are you doing?" a shrill voice called towards me. "Don't think you can go in and steal anything from that office."

I turned around and was totally and completely not surprised to be face to face with Cindy. She, however, was surprised to see that it was me under the bike helmet. Her eyes opened wide before they narrowed at me again.

"Oh, it's you," she said. "Were you going to try to steal the security tapes to try and cover up the murder for your best friend?"

"What do you know about the security tapes?" I asked, hoping she didn't know what Mandy had actually been doing during the time of the murder.

"Mr. Parks told me that he had turned in the tapes to the police and said that he had told Bill and Sally about them," Cindy said. "Naturally I figured that meant your friend was guilty and he was trying to give her and her parents a heads up so that you could once again cover it up or frame someone else or run to Mexico or something."

I breathed a sigh of relief. So far Cindy had no idea that Mandy had been the one to destroy her bicycle. She also didn't seem to know about Louise having turned herself in for questioning. I certainly wasn't going to be the bearer of bad news or of any news for Cindy, so I grabbed my bike and put the kickstand up.

"Cindy, Mandy was not the person who killed Hilda," I said. "I'm sorry that you lost your friend. It is a horrible situation. But what I am doing right now is trying to get to the bottom of it so that we can know once and for all what happened."

A few raindrops started to fall as the daily rain shower started. It was so warm out that the rain felt more like bathwater than the cold rain that usually fell in Minnesota. Cindy's mouth puckered into a scowl and she opened her mouth to say something before clamping it shut again.

Climbing up onto my bicycle seat, I gave Cindy a little wave and pushed off, trying to get back to the RV before the rain picked up. I enjoy a warm rain but not when it absolutely drenches me. After a short while, I realized that I definitely would not make it home in time for this rain so I cycled up to the Candy Cane Palace, parking myself and my bicycle under an awning.

It was peaceful sitting there alone, watching the rain fall. A wave of calm washed over me as I let myself soak up the vacation feeling I had been missing for most of this trip. Letting my mind wander, I wondered if Trevor had proposed yet. When I thought of a proposal I usually thought of evening, like popping the question during a beautiful sunset. But a brunch proposal didn't seem totally unusual.

Of course, my mind naturally wandered to Max and what he thought about the timing of proposals. I got that giddy, butterfly feeling again as I pictured us on a romantic sunset walk around Shady Lake in the middle of a warm summer evening. I imagined him getting down on one knee and opening up a ring box, asking for my hand in marriage.

I squealed a little squeal to myself, glad that no one was around to actually hear it. As much as I loved Max, I didn't feel the need to announce my school-girl self to the people around me.

The rain was still falling pretty hard, but I could see the clouds were starting to move on. I wouldn't be stuck under this awning for much longer. Then out of the corner of my eye, I saw someone out and about in the rain shower.

Someone clad in a big red poncho was riding a bike towards the entrance to the park. I watched, wondering what was so important that they had to come out in the rain. But instead of going out the gate, they turned and parked their bike in front of the park office.

Now I was intrigued. Could the mystery cyclist be Tom? Maybe I'd be able to see the tapes now, provided I ran through the rain. That didn't make any sense because why would he have abandoned his golf cart to ride through the rain in a poncho?

As the person turned around, I sucked in my breath. Susie was looking out from underneath the hood of the poncho. I wasn't sure what she was doing but by the way she was looking around, she didn't want anyone to see what she was doing. Thankfully, I was hidden up next to the building and under the awning so even though I saw her eyes dart this way, Susie didn't seem to see me.

The rain kept on falling as Susie carefully scanned the park once, twice, three times. No one else was crazy enough to be out in the rain, especially because these showers never seemed to last very long. Most people would just wait the ten minutes or so until the rain shower moved on and they could get out to get on with their day. Whatever Susie was planning, she would have to do it fast before the rain stopped.

Finally, Susie must have decided it was safe because she turned around and bent down, fiddling with the doorknob until the door popped open and she disappeared inside. I stayed huddled against the wall, wondering what in the world she could be doing in there.

I didn't have to wonder long because as fast as she had gone in, Susie was back out, shutting the door behind her. She wasn't holding anything and by the look on her face, it was because she hadn't found whatever it was she was looking for.

Susie climbed on her bicycle and rode out of sight, back in the direction of her trailer. A minute later, the rain lightened up and then stopped all together. I stood up and grabbed my bicycle, ready to head back to the RV. Before I could go anywhere, I spotted a police cruiser coming in the entrance to the park. They drove slowly through the park and as I watched, they drove straight to Bill and Sally's driveway. Uh-oh, this couldn't be good.

•Chapter Twenty-Seven•

The biggest advantage of having a bicycle instead of walking was that I was able to get back to the trailer before the police officers even got out of the car. I skidded my bicycle to a stop on the grass next to the driveway, tipping over but catching myself before I fell onto the ground. Flipping out the kickstand, I parked my bike and hoped the cops weren't here to get Mandy even though I was pretty sure they were.

"Hello Officer Mendoza, Officer Johnson," I said with a wave. "Beautiful morning! What brings you back here today?"

Officer Johnson muttered a hello and stared blankly at me. His beady eyes were locked on me, always seeming to be filing away information about his surroundings. He seemed almost like a very perceptive rat. Officer Mendoza was a bit more pleasant which may be because he seemed to actually have a personality behind his badge. He took his sunglasses off and hung them on his shirt pocket, which was level with my eyeline. Officer Mendoza was so tall that he shaded me nicely from the sun, which was rapidly warming up.

"Good morning Miss Schmidt," he said with a smile. "It is a lovely morning. Honestly, this is what almost every morning is like down here. It is what keeps me here in Florida."

"I completely understand that," I said with a big smile, wondering if he ignored my question about why they were here or just didn't answer it. I decided to take another stab at it. "Are you just coming to check in about Hilda's case?"

"Ma'am, would you please let us get back to our business?" Officer Johnson said.

"You're in luck because I'm also staying here, so I'll let you guys in," I said.

Walking up to the trailer, I unbuckled my helmet and hoped that my hair didn't look too wild. I didn't want them to think I was a weirdo even though I guess I kind of was one. Who else would investigate a murder in their spare time?

I opened the door to the sunroom and called for Mandy to come out. Trevor was probably back at his hotel sleeping, but Mandy was taking advantage of the fact that she was not only on vacation but also released from police custody, for now at least.

The officers both followed me into the sun room, but refused to sit down when I offered them a seat. Officer Mendoza declined with a polite shake of his head while Officer Johnson just stared at me. I wondered if their contrasting personalities helped them on the job or not. Kind of like a good cop, bad cop thing except they were friendly cop and lump-on-a-log cop.

Bill came out of the camper first, his face set in a stern expression with his eyebrows furrowed. If the cops were coming for his baby girl again, he wanted the men to know that they'd have to go through him first. Sally came next, immediately scurrying towards the bar area to make up a plate of snacks. Was it the Minnesotan in her that decided she had to provide food and drinks to everyone, even the police officers who may be coming to arrest her daughter? I had to think it contributed because every woman over the age of thirty back in Minnesota seemed to move to snack preparation almost on overdrive when someone came over.

Last of all was Mandy, who came out dressed in a pair of knee-length khaki shorts and a purple tank top with a gold lace design on the front. She had been so excited this morning to finally start her vacation and now here we were meeting with the police once again. The sad expression on her face tugged on my heartstrings and I hoped that no matter what happened, Mandy would come out the other side happy.

"Ma'am, we will have to take you back down to the station again," Officer Johnson said.

"But you said she was basically cleared as a suspect in the murder," Bill said, his voice booming without actually shouting. "What in the world are you going to take her in for now?"

Sally walked over with a plate of lemon bars in one hand, putting her other hand on Bill's shoulder. While we couldn't do much to prevent them from taking Mandy in, we could try to keep Bill calm enough to not be arrested for obstructing a police investigation. Officer Mendoza took a lemon bar off of the plate, smiling with thanks at Sally while Officer Johnson stared at the plate like Sally was trying to poison them.

"After reviewing the security footage from the park on the night of the murder, we now have questions about a different crime that was reported that night," Officer Johnson said. "We will be taking her in right now."

"I think it would be better for everyone if Mandy came along without much of a scene," Officer Mendoza said gently. "There is no need for handcuffs or brute force. The crime we are going to question her about is nothing as serious as murder and honestly, this crime means that she is officially not a suspect in the murder of Hilda."

I breathed out a small sigh of relief. I couldn't do anything about the stupid decision Mandy made to destroy Cindy's bicycle, but at least she wasn't a murder suspect anymore.

Mandy was standing near the door to the trailer staring at the ground, nervously rubbing her arms. I walked across the sunroom and wrapped her n a big hug. I squeezed her tight, hoping it wouldn't be long before she was back with us again.

"I'll talk to Trevor," I said quietly.

"He's going to be so upset at me for this," Mandy said, her eyes filling with tears. "It was such a stupid thing to do and he came down to surprise me and here I am being the one to ruin it this time."

"Everyone makes mistakes," I said. "Usually it's me, so I think you are due to be the one to flub it all up."

Mandy laughed and wiped the tears away. She couldn't argue with that. For once, I got to help her out of a jam of her own making.

After a hug from both of her parents, Mandy followed Officer Johnson and Officer Mendoza out of the sun room and down to the police car, where she slid into the backseat. As they backed out of the driveway, Mandy waved at us with a small, hopeful smile on her face.

Bill and Sally were standing together, their arms around each other's shoulders. They watched the car drive away with Mandy in the back and in that moment, their love for each other seemed to be what kept them standing upright. Besides my own parents, Bill and Sally were the other couple that I longed to emulate. Through everything, they turned to each other and supported each other.

"She will get through this," I said to them.

"Mandy is so strong and even though she made a mistake, she will make it right again."

Sally sniffled as they both nodded at me. I would have to be the one to call Trevor and explain that good news, his girlfriend isn't a murder suspect anymore but bad news, now she was being questioned for vandalism and we all know that she actually did it. I grabbed a lemon bar out of the sunroom and went into the trailer to call Trevor.

•Chapter Twenty-Eight•

"Go fish," Trevor said, taking a large bite out of another lemon bar. Each time Sally offered the plate of bars around, Trevor grabbed one. By now, he must have eaten at least five and I'm not sure if he was stress eating or if this was just his normal rate of goodie consumption. It was so distracting that I had actually stopped myself from taking more than one lemon bar because I was curious just how many Trevor would eat.

Bill, Sally, Trevor, and I were sitting on the deck trying to take our minds off of Mandy being gone by playing the simplest card game we could. She had been at the police station for almost two hours now and we hadn't heard anything from her. Trevor had rushed over as soon as I told him what had happened and just as I thought, he was not upset with Mandy at all. Instead, he was just worried about how she was doing now that she was in police custody again.

While we had hoped to be distracted by the card game, it was turning out to be the other way around. One simple round of Go Fish had taken us almost an hour because we kept losing track of whose turn it was.

Then Bill's phone rang and the deck turned

into a circus. After he managed to pull the smartphone out of his pocket, he was so jittery that he couldn't hit the button. Before he could try again, Sally tried to grab the phone out of his hand and answer it herself except instead she just managed to knock it to the floor of the deck. Trevor grabbed for it and was finally the one to answer. I simply sat back and watched the whole spectacle.

"Hello, Mr. Bill's phone," Trevor said while Bill rolled his eyes. Trevor smiled and pointed at the phone while he whispered to us. "It's Mandy."

Trevor nodded a few times, his smile growing wider and wider. He jumped out of his chair, accidentally bumping the table and sending the playing cards flying. Bill managed to grab the plate of lemon bars before they slid off to their demise. Sally and I started to gather up the cards.

"Of course, I'll be right there to pick you up," Trevor said. "I love you and I will see you soon."

Trevor punched the hand holding the phone up in the air in victory. Bill jumped forward to grab the phone out of his hand, like he was afraid the next step of Trevor's victory dance might be spiking it to the ground. Sally grabbed my hands in hers and squeezed them, her face shining with happiness.

"Here's what I think we should do," Sally said, breaking away from me. "Bill and I will stay back and prepare a special dinner to celebrate having Mandy back again. Tessa, you go with Trevor. Now everyone put a smile on your face and let's celebrate."

I nodded and dashed inside to grab my purse. When I came back out, Trevor and Sally were having a whispered conversation while Bill puttered around arranging things on the deck while he used up his nervous, excited energy.

"Come on Tessa," Trevor said. "Let's go! Hop in the convertible and let's go pick up our girl."

Sally winked at Trevor as we headed down the stairs and towards the red convertible. I walked around the back of the car and Trevor was so excited that he jumped over the driver's side door into his seat. I giggled as I climbed in and buckled up.

After a fast drive with the wind blowing through our hair, we pulled up outside of the police station. It was still the same, non-descript building it was before but this time Mandy wasn't outside to greet us so we would have to venture inside.

Trevor parked the car and practically skipped through the parking lot. That was something I never thought I would see. The more time I spent with Trevor, the less he seemed like a lazy skaterboy.

Inside the front doors of the police station, Trevor made a beeline to the front desk to ask a very bored looking woman about Mandy. The woman picked up a phone and pointed to the hard plastic chairs that we were supposed to sit in and wait. I took a seat, but Trevor was too jumpy and nervous to sit down so he paced back and forth.

After a few minutes, a door opened and Mandy came out followed by Officer Mendoza. He towered over her, but the large smile on his face made him seem instantly less scary looking. Trevor flew over to Mandy, picking her up in his arms and twirling her around. Her face was so happy and she threw her head back as she laughed happily. Officer Mendoza smiled at the happy scene and I was glad he had been the one to accompany Mandy out instead of Officer Johnson.

"Let me walk you all outside," Officer Mendoza said, throwing a friendly wave to the crabby lady at the front desk. She couldn't help but smile and wave back at the happy police officer.

As we walked out the doors, the warm sunshine hit us and for a moment everything felt right. For just that moment, I could put the murder out of my mind and soak in the excitement of Mandy's release. But I just had to know what in the world happened with the vandalism charge.

"I'm so glad that everything worked out," Officer Mendoza said. "You've been through enough in the last few days."

"Thank you so much for everything," Mandy said. She was absolutely beaming, mostly at Trevor.

"Wait a minute, what exactly happened?" I

asked. "Mandy, do you need to pay a fine or something?"

Mandy giggled and Officer Mendoza let out a loud guffaw. They glanced at each other like they were hiding some sort of secret.

"Well, in an instance like this, we would usually have the person pay a fine that is equal in value to the property they destroyed," Officer Mendoza said. "And since Mandy already replaced the original bicycle with a bicycle of greater value, there isn't much we can do. I did strongly suggest that Mandy write a very heavily heartfelt apology letter."

"Officer Mendoza, did you meet Cindy?" Trevor asked. "I'm not totally sure, but I don't think she is going to accept that."

A vision flew through my mind of Mandy down on her knees literally begging Cindy for forgiveness for that stupid bike. Even if Mandy decided to do that, I don't think Cindy would accept it. She didn't even want to accept the brand new bicycle.

"Either way, I'm hoping this is the last time we have to bring you into the station," Officer Mendoza said.

"We are all hoping that," I said.

Officer Mendoza handed me his card, telling me to call if we needed anything else. After a few more goodbyes and thank yous, Officer Mendoza

walked back into the police station and Mandy and I
started towards the convertible. Trevor didn't follow,
instead pacing a bit on the sidewalk and kicking the
rocks he came across.

Mandy and I paused halfway to the car and
looked at each other. We had known each other so
long that we could talk without talking and right now
we were both saying we had no idea what Trevor was
doing or why. With an exasperated sigh from me and
a shoulder shrug from Mandy, we headed back
towards the police station.

The closer we got to Trevor, the more nervous
he looked. He was sweating, but I don't think it was
from the heat. He was walking back and forth in front
of the door and glancing at Mandy and back at the
ground.

"Trevor, I think we should get back to the RV
park, don't you think?" Mandy said sweetly.

"Umm yeah, we will but I just really wanted to
go to the beach today," Trevor said. "And I know that
there is a beach just two blocks that way so let's just
walk over there."

"Shouldn't we wait until it is not nearing
evening and we have swimsuits to actually swim?" I
asked.

Trevor turned and looked at me like he had
just remembered I was there. He narrowed his eyes at
me like he was confused, not actually sure what I was

talking about. I stared back at him, wondering why he was being so weird.

"Okay honey, let's go to the beach," Mandy said, putting her arm through his arm.

I used my telepathy to ask her what in the world was happening, but the message she sent back to me told me she had no idea what was going on. I had an inkling about what was happening, but I guess I'd have to wait and see.

•Chapter Twenty-Nine•

We walked past a few half-filled parking lots and an autobody shop before we came to a tiny path leading to a very small, mostly rocky beach. There was a restaurant on one end of the beach and a fishing pier on the other end. It was maybe only twenty feet across and, if I was right about what we were actually doing here, it was not the kind of beach Trevor had been hoping it was.

The sun was starting to set over the horizon and while the beach wasn't the most beautiful, it had a great view of the sunset. I wished Max was here and that we could be sitting on the deck of that restaurant eating a romantic dinner while we watched the sun go down.

"Mandy, maybe you want to go on a little walk with me down by the water?" Trevor said as he cleared his throat. "Tessa, maybe you could watch from, uh, over there."

"Sure, that sounds lovely," Mandy said.

I looked to where Trevor was pointing and saw a gross, moss covered rock where I was apparently supposed to wait. I did not take his suggestion, but I did find a small spot on the sand where I could sit down and be alone with my thoughts. Mandy set her purse down next to me and took Trevor's outstretched hand.

Walking up and down the beachfront, Mandy and Trevor couldn't take their eyes off of each other. Sparks of love were flying back and forth between them. I envied the fact that they got to spend this vacation together even if most of the time had actually been spent apart.

Trevor had one hand intertwined with Mandy's but his other hand was deep in his pocket. Looking closer at his pocket, I spotted what I already knew was there. A small cube shape made a barely noticeable lump in his pocket. Ah ha! I'm not sure that this was what Trevor had in mind for his proposal, but he was making it work.

As the sun got lower and the sky became more colorful and more beautiful, I could see Trevor talking to Mandy. She was blushing, but in the sort of way that she was hearing the sort of compliments that she wasn't sure how to take. I'd have to ask her later what Trevor was saying because so far, apart from the scenery, he seemed to be nailing this proposal.

On the next go-around, Trevor slowed down and then stopped in the middle of the beach. He grabbed both of Mandy's hands, holding them tenderly. They had somehow stopped with the setting sun perfectly centered between them.

'This would be a perfect picture,' I thought to myself. 'Wait a minute, I could be the one to take the picture.'

My flip phone was not ideal for picture taking, but I pulled it out and grabbed a quick, grainy picture of them with the sun between them. It was nowhere near perfect, but it would have to do. Flip phones don't come with a great camera for whatever reason. I wished I could take a better picture because the colors in the sky were the most beautiful I'd ever seen.

That's when I spotted Mandy's purse next to my feet. While Mandy can be a bit of a smartphone addict, I was pretty sure it would be somewhere in her bottomless purse. I just had to find it first.

Mandy's purse was one of those large totes that she seemed to carry her life around in. I couldn't really judge because I usually carried one that size also. I rummaged around, feeling for the phone and mostly pulling out old gum wrappers and various packages of gum in different flavors. Someone really needed to talk to that girl about her ridiculous gum habit.

Finally, I felt her phone in the very bottom of her bag and I pulled it out triumphantly. I swiped over to the camera and started snapping away, hitting different parts of the screen to pull the right amount of light in. Back when I was Big-City Tessa, I used to run a beautifully curated social media feed and apparently I still had what it took to take a good picture with a smartphone.

I clicked on and on and on as Trevor finally got down on one knee and pulled the ring box out of his pocket. As he opened it, Mandy put her hands over her mouth and while I couldn't see her face very clearly, I knew she was crying tears of happiness.

After Trevor said a few things, I could see Mandy nod her head yes and lean down to kiss Trevor. He took the ring out of the box and slid it onto her finger. Popping up from his kneeling position, he scooped her up in his arms again, kissing her hard on the mouth.

A cheer went up from both the fishing pier and the restaurant where the curious onlookers were enjoying the positive outcome of the strange proposal at the beach that wasn't really a beach. I cheered along with them, excited to finally see Mandy get her happily ever after.

The sun was still setting, slipping quickly over the horizon. Watching the happy couple as they took in the dregs of the day, I felt a twinge of loneliness. I took out my phone and sent a quick message to Max. It was a bit more difficult considering my hands were all bandaged up.

Just watched Trevor and Mandy get engaged. Now I'm watching a beautiful sunset. Both of these things made me miss you. I love you.

My phone buzzed right away with a message back from Max.

I love you too. I wish I was there watching the sunset, except I would be watching the beautiful girl beside me instead. :)

I smiled and even though I was still alone, I didn't feel lonely. Vacation was fun but I couldn't wait to be back in Max's arms. Minnesota might be cold and snowy, but it had Max which meant it would always be home.

Mandy and Trevor were headed back up the beach toward me. I stood up and Mandy scampered toward me, holding out her left hand toward me. I grabbed it and took a good look at the ring. Good engagement rings come in all shapes and sizes, so I was ready to ooh and ahh over a tiny diamond but I was very impressed with not only the large size of the diamond, but also the tasteful setting that made it look beautiful instead of gaudy.

"Nice job Trevor," I said, elbowing him a bit in the ribs.

Trevor was grinning like an idiot but for once it wasn't grating on my nerves. This time there was excitement behind his smile rather than the stupidity I normally sensed. I couldn't help but smile back, mirroring his happiness.

"Let's get back to the trailer," Trevor said. "Your mom and dad have been busy making us a special dinner to celebrate. Everyone back to the convertible!"

All three of us laughed and headed back to the car. My happiness was bubbling up and spilling over the top. I couldn't wait to help Mandy plan her wedding, especially because she had helped me plan my wedding to Peter. I couldn't help but wonder if she would be helping me plan my wedding to Max soon.

•Chapter Thirty•

Trevor drove the convertible right up to the end of the driveway and we were surprised to see a whole crowd of people waiting for us on the deck. Bill and Sally had taken the opportunity to make it a party instead of just a celebration dinner. A cheer went up as Mandy hopped out of the car and met her mother at the top of the deck stairs.

I grabbed our purses and climbed out of the car. Trevor went to park in guest parking while I approached the throng of women currently vying to see the engagement ring. All of the Dolls and their husbands had shown up for the celebration party along with some of the other neighbors. The ladies were all taking turns grabbing Mandy's hand and cooing over the amazing ring Trevor had picked out. Trevor came bounding back up the road and was immediately met with slaps on the back from the guys and hugs from the ladies.

Puttering around the party, I was drawn into conversation after conversation about everything from Minnesota, which is where most of the RV park residents seemed to be from, to the engagement at the weird beach. Everyone also asked me about my hands since they were all bandaged up like a mummy. One thing that was not a topic of conversation was Hilda's murder. In a way I understood not wanting to ruin the party with talk of death, but it seemed more like everyone was purposely ignoring it and that didn't feel right for poor Hilda.

Mandy was all smiles as she was seated like a queen on her throne, entertaining person after person who took a turn to congratulate her and make some small talk. Trevor was standing next to her chair, occasionally bending down to kiss her or hold her hand for a moment while he entertained his own guests.

I heard a golf cart pulling up to the party and I was happy to see that it was Tom Parks. Maybe I could talk him into letting me watch those security tapes now. Passing through the party crowd to get to him wouldn't be easy though. Bill and Sally knew everyone and invited everyone to celebrate with them.

Karen and Kathy each grabbed me by an arm suddenly and started talking over each other. The only way I could tell them apart was by looking at their pins, but they were standing so close to me and talking so fast that I couldn't sneak a glance and just had to guess who was who without saying their names.

"We just saw those pictures you took," KathyKaren said. "They were wonderful!"

"Did you really just take those with a phone?"
213

KarenKathy said. "I can't believe technology these days. We used to have to tote around a big ole camera with film in it."

"And we had to use it all up and take it to get developed before we could actually see the pictures," KathyKaren said. "There wasn't even one-hour picture at that point."

The sisters talked back and forth about how much technology had advanced and how my generation would never know how lucky they were even though I kind of did because I vividly remember bringing a disposable film camera to summer camp with me.

After a few more back and forths with compliments on the photos which I demurely tried to pass off as just good luck because if they had seen the beach we ended up at and the beautiful sunset, they would have known it was pure luck that they turned out so well.

I was just trying to cross the crowded party deck to get to Tom who, by this point, was sitting in the sunroom with a crowd of the husbands and other men from the park. Every time I managed to take a few more steps, I was stopped by another Doll to compliment me on the pictures and ask what in the world happened to my hands. I started to feel legitimately bad about all of the compliments because other than the fact that I tapped the screen a few times to focus the light, I didn't do much else to take good pictures.

Marie jingled up with armfuls of bracelets. She kept gesturing around with excitement and she jingled so much that it reminded me of Christmas. Lynn caught me next and insisted on giving me a big hug. She was so short that I had to lean my head back to avoid getting a mouthful of her beehive.

The Dolls were an eccentric group, but I had to admit that they were really growing on me. They were just all so sincere and loving. It wasn't even my engagement but with my tangential link to the major life event, they were roping me in to congratulate me also. It was odd and also incredibly sweet.

There were only two Dolls who hadn't congratulated me: Louise and Susie. I understood why Louise hadn't talked to me. Even though everyone was steering around the topic of the murder and all of the suspects, I knew that Louise was still being held in custody.

Susie, however, was at the party but it almost seemed like she was avoiding me. I had accidentally locked eyes with her at one point as I was attempting to cross the deck and while I smiled and waved, she had looked away. While I otherwise would assume she hadn't seen me, it was just a beat too long to think that. I wasn't sure what was going on with her but I wondered if it had to do with what I had seen yesterday. Susie hadn't seemed to see me, but maybe she knew I had been around when she broke into the office.

Either way, I did try to wave at her one more time when I reached the door to the sunroom and was about to go inside. This time Susie was part of the crowd admiring Mandy's ring so when I waved, everyone waved back including Susie. She was the only one who did with a partial scowl though.

Pulling open the door to the sunroom, I realized this was very much like the parties my parents would throw where even though everyone started out together, eventually the men and women would all separate to do different things.

The sunroom was full of men, most of them probably husbands of the women outside. They looked a bit out of place in the wicker furniture and floral cushions that were scattered around the room, but it didn't phase them down at all. Laughter and conversation were flowing through the room as old rock and roll was playing on the stereo.

As I entered, there was raucous laughter coming from a few different small groups around the room and I stopped just inside the door to try and pinpoint where Tom was without looking too out of place. My eyes scanned over the crowd, looking for the round, bald man. It was a bit more difficult here where Tom's description fit almost half of the crowd of men.

"Tessa!" Bill stood up from one of the groups and shouted my name. "Come on over here and celebrate with us."

I made my way through the maze of furniture until I reached the far corner of the room where Bill was holding court on a large wicker peacock chair. I could tell by his friendly roar that he had already been celebrating a bit with a few glasses of whiskey, which I knew was his celebration drink.

One of the men stood and I was given the chair next to Bill. Sinking down into the cushions, I glanced around the crowd and was happy to see that Tom was sitting just two chairs to the left of me. I wasn't sure how I was going to ask him about the tapes, but at least now I was close to him.

"Here you go Tessa, take a drink with me," Bill roared. His jowly cheeks were red from the alcohol and I had to laugh. Bill was not one to have too much to drink but he was taking his celebration seriously today.

Bill was holding a glass of whiskey out to me. I was normally a wine drinker but I wasn't going to look a gift horse in the mouth. Knowing Bill, this was some sort of super special whiskey that he had been saving for a celebration.

I took the glass out of his hand and took a sip. I had to hold it in both hands since the bandages made it hard to hold one-handed. It must be a good whiskey because it was pretty smooth, but still also pretty burny on my throat. Apparently, I would never be mature enough to actually appreciate a good whiskey.

"Tessa, thank you so much for everything you've ever done for Mandy," Bill said. His eyes got a little watery. "You have been the sister we were never able to give her. And now you've helped her not go to prison. So thank you. We really do owe you a lot."

"To Tessa!" someone behind me said.

"To Tessa!" everyone chimed in as they all held their glasses aloft.

Many cheers went around as they drank to me. I used both hands raise my glass in thanks and accepted it with a nod of my head before I took a long swig. It still burned, but I supposed I could classify it as a 'good burn.'

The men fell back into normal chatter and I was pleased to watch the man to my left stand up and leave. Before someone else could sit down, I slid over so that I was next to Tom. This was my chance to ask him and judging by his pink cheeks, he would be more susceptible to saying yes to me.

"Hello Mr. Parks, I actually had a question for you," I said. "I believe you said you still had copies of the security tapes in the park office? Would you mind terribly if I came by sometime and just took a little peek at them? I would love to just see what the police are seeing."

"Oh Tessa, you've been so lovely since you've been here," Tom said, his voice slurring just a little. "Here's my key. Why don't you run down there now and check them out. I normally wouldn't give out my keys to just anyone, but Bill and Sally trust you, so I trust you. As long as you weren't the one who broke in the other day."

"Oh no, I would never," I said. "Someone broke in? Was anything taken?"

"That's the strange part," he said. "I figured someone broke in for the petty cash, but besides rummaging around a bit in my mess, nothing was taken. I thought it was pretty odd."

Tom looked off in the distance as he mulled over the strange break-in, but he was quickly drawn into another conversation with the man seated on the other side of him.

Nothing had been taken from the office. Whatever Susie had been looking for was either not there or hidden when she broke in yesterday. I took the keys from Mr. Parks, promised I would be back soon and started the fight back through the party and down to my bicycle. I had something very specific I wanted to look for, I just hoped I could find it.

•Chapter Thirty-One•

I unlocked the door of the park office and marveled at just how small it actually was. When I peeked inside the other day it looked small, but being inside was a different story. For one thing, the roof was peaked and anyone taller than average would only be able to stand up in the very middle of the shed.

There was a desk covered in paperwork in the very center of the shed. On one side was a very narrow bookshelf that held binders of what must be park documents. On the back wall of the shed was a shelf with all of the equipment for the security system. Before I left the party, Mr. Parks said that he had put all of the tapes for the night of the murder right on top of the VHS player when he came back from the police department. I rifled through them and found one that looked promising.

A small, ancient television sat on the shelf, the kind with the VHS player built right in. While I understood that this was a trailer park for retirees, I marveled that they still depended on technology this old. The tape I wanted to watch was labeled "Candy Cane Palace Patio." I popped it in and pressed play.

The tape started out quite a while before the murder, so I looked around for the remote. I spotted it attached to the side of the TV and grabbed it off. The camera was trained mostly on the door to go into the Candy Cane Palace but in the corner of the screen, the bushes from around the pool area could just barely be seen. The gate to the pool was just out of camera range. I fast-forwarded through a lot of the beginning, watching dressed-up people walking to the dance. I even managed to spot Mandy, Bill, Sally, and I all heading inside.

Once I spotted Hilda and Cindy going into the dance, I pressed play. They hadn't been at the dance for very long before they caused trouble, so I watched from then on. A short time later they came back out but instead of leaving together, they stopped outside on the patio and had a short conversation. Cindy seemed to be telling Hilda to go to the pool. I knew that Cindy had instructed her underling to go make notes on all of the things Bill hadn't done that night. Then the two women split up and while I couldn't see Hilda in the pool area, I did see her head towards the gate.

Next up I saw Louise come out of the dance. She seemed to be going for a casual walk, maybe to clear her head after the confrontation with Cindy, but then she suddenly stopped. Louise was looking in the direction of the pool and she must have spotted Hilda. The video was too grainy to get a good look at her face, so I couldn't get a sense of what she was thinking.

Louise disappeared into the pool area and a short time later she appeared back on the screen, visibly distraught just as Susie was coming out of the Candy Cane Palace. Susie jogged up to Louise and put her arm around Louise's shoulder, escorting her off screen and back to her trailer.

In the interim, Mandy exited the dance and dashed off camera. I knew she had already formulated her plan to destroy Cindy's bike at that point and she would sneak off to get it and bring it to the dumpster area where she managed to tear it apart. Bill came out after her and looked around, not sure where Mandy had gone. He also dashed off screen, looking for Mandy.

I figured the next thing I would see would be the Dolls and I coming out of the dance, but it wasn't. It was so fast that I almost missed it, but someone walked by and into the pool area. It was someone who wasn't coming from the dance, but had come from somewhere in the park I rewound and played the tape a few times, trying to make out who it was, but I couldn't quite tell. Whoever it was had short hair and upon further inspection, may have been wearing some sort of necklace. Unfortunately, the direction they came from meant I mostly saw the back of their head as they went by.

Shortly after the head disappeared into the

pool area, I saw the Dolls coming out of the dance followed by me. We didn't stay on the patio long, hurriedly scurrying off to look for Susie and Louise. I remember that we didn't think we would need to check the patio area or the pool and now I was horrified to realize that whatever happened to Hilda was probably happening as we passed right by the pool.

Our search party quickly split up and ran off in different directions to search the park. Then there was some downtime where nothing seemed to be happening, but then the head appeared again. This time they were going in the opposite direction and I could kind of see their face, but the grainy VHS quality made it hard to tell who it was.

Again, I rewound and re-watched that face going by to see if I could see any details. The only problem was the depending on when I paused it, the fuzzy black and white pause lines that came with the ancient VHS technology would cover parts of the person. It looked like whoever it was had fallen into the pool because their short hair seemed like it was dripping water. Hilda was found in the pool so perhaps she had struggled with this person before she died.

I kept trying, pausing it at different milliseconds to try and get the clearest picture I could. Finally, I hit the jackpot. The grainy pause lines were going just above and below the mystery person. Leaning in close to the TV, I tried to see more of the person's face but unfortunately the only thing I go was that they were an older woman which made sense seeing how the murder occurred in an RV park for retirees. That described half of the population.

Instead, I focused on the necklace. It was a simple chain with some sort of charm on it. Most of the women here wore a necklace like that, so I tried my hardest to make out what it was. There were two small circles, so maybe they were interlocking rings? If there was just one circle, I would assume it said MOM but maybe it spelled out a different word.

I kicked back in the chair and studied the necklace. The problem was that all of the women wore jewelry here, even in the pool. It was a way to show off their hobbies, their kids and grandkids, or even how long they had been married. The jewelry didn't have to be big or expensive to be a status symbol.

Suddenly it all clicked. I knew who was in the video. Sitting up, I almost fell over in the desk chair as I scrambled to get my phone out of my pocket. I took out my phone and Officer Mendoza's business card and punched the number into the phone.

"Hello, Officer Mendoza," he said.

"Hi Officer Mendoza," I said. "This is Tessa Schmidt, Mandy's friend. I was just looking at the security tapes from the night of Hilda's murder and I think I know who did it."

I told Officer Mendoza everything I had figured out from watching the grainy tape and then I held my breath. While I was glad I had been able to contact him instead of Officer Johnson, it still didn't mean that he would believe me.

"Well, that is certainly interesting," Officer Mendoza said. "And I think you might be right. We've been working on those tapes but we hadn't noticed that detail yet."

"I also have a plan, if you are willing to listen," I said.

Together, Officer Mendoza and I hashed out a plan to catch the culprit in their tracks. It wasn't quite the same as working with Max, but I got the feeling the Officer Mendoza and I might get to be real friends.

•Chapter Thirty-Two•

I was up bright and early with the sun the next morning. I tried to lay with my eyes shut for a while, but sleep was elusive. Even though I had been competently riding my bicycle around the park, I was still a bit nervous about riding with the Bike Brigade today. Even after practicing on the bike with my hands all bandaged up, I still knew I would have to focus as I rode. As long as I didn't squeeze the handlebars too tight and my bandages were thick enough to pad my poor burnt palms, my hands were fine. I also had some butterflies in my stomach from the plan I had to come up with to catch the killer. As long as Officer Mendoza and I both played our parts, everything would go fine, but I had still been up almost all night thinking about it.

The one thing I needed to remember was to not tell Officer Johnson that I had come up with the plan. Apparently he was not just utterly forgettable, but he was also the type to adhere exactly to the rules and I'm assuming there were plenty of rules about not letting civilians make plans to catch killers, even if they had been the one to figure out the crime. I liked Officer Mendoza enough that I wasn't going to get him in trouble.

The bike ride was scheduled to start at eleven,

which gave us an hour to ride to our destination where we would have a picnic lunch to celebrate the bike riding season. This was the time of year that many of the snowbirds started to migrate home after winter, so it was a fun farewell sort of event. There was even supposed to be some fun games and a raffle to win a few prizes. Normally it would be a relaxing event, but today was going to be a little bit different.

I wanted to have someone come with me, but no one else wanted to go for a long bike ride and I couldn't actually tell them what was going to happen with the plan and everything, so I knew I would have to do this alone. First, I wanted to send a message to Max.

Hey Max, just wanted to say I love you and I hope you have a good day.

If I told Max my plan, I knew he would do everything in his power to talk me out of it. At least when I was in Shady Lake, he was around to help me with my crazy plans, but there was no way I would be able to convince him that I knew what I was doing. So I made the decision to not tell him until it was over.

Even though Max was working, he was usually able to send a quick message back. Today was no different as my phone buzzed almost instantly.

Hey Sweet Thing, I love you too. Have a great bike ride.

I needed to do something to distract myself until it was time for the bike ride, so I took my stack of trashy magazines out to the deck along with some breakfast and flipped through them as I fueled up for the ride. Losing myself in the world of celebrity gossip was all too easy and when I looked at my phone, I realized it was almost time to start the ride. If I didn't skedaddle, they would leave without me and the plan would be ruined.

Tossing all of my magazines into my suitcase, I grabbed the bike helmet and shoved it on my head, clicking the buckle under my chin. As I climbed on the bicycle seat and pushed off, I couldn't help trying to get myself into the right mindset.

"It's go time," I whispered to myself before I started laughing hysterically at just what a dope I was. I took a few deep breaths to calm down and re-center myself. I couldn't be weird or emotional if I wanted to catch a killer.

I joined the large group of bicycles at the entrance gate. I had been told there were two rules to be part of the Bike Brigade: Everyone had to wear a helmet and everyone had to wear a red shirt. I was a rule follower, so check and check.

The Bike Brigade was much bigger than I expected and several dozen park residents and their bicycles were waiting at the park entrance. I was a bit tickled to see a handful of couples even had two-seater bicycles. Maybe I could talk Max into riding one of those with me. The sea of red bicycle riders milled around until finally Susie climbed up onto a rock that was in the grass next to the paved road. She cupped her hands around her mouth and shouted out directions to everyone.

"Hello everyone, I'm so glad you could join us today," she said. "Everyone seems to be following the rules of the club so let me just say that it looks like great weather for our picnic and if everyone rides safely, it will be a great day."

There was a smattering of cheers and clapping before everyone climbed on their bicycles. I hadn't actually gotten off of my bike so I scooted around everyone, hoping to stay towards the front of the pack during the ride. The best bet for our plan to work was if I could stay up front, which would be a challenge both mentally and physically for me, not to mention having to try not to focus on my poor hands.

Susie was the leader of the Bike Brigade and she planned the routes so once she shoved off and started pedaling, the rest of the Brigade followed along. I ended up just a few spots back from the front, which would be great. The beginning of the ride was along a semi-busy highway, so we all went single file to make sure no one was too close to the cars that were whizzing past. In Minnesota, everyone looked out for bike riders and gave them space but apparently that wasn't the case in all states. Score another for Minnesota.

I tried to keep a slow, steady pace so that I wouldn't burn out my leg muscles right away. There wasn't much I could do until we were done riding in one big line. I was pleased to find out that I wasn't puttering out as fast as I thought I would. Once I was back in Minnesota and the snow melted, I thought maybe I would buy a bike.

Susie signaled a turn and just like a group of synchronized swimmers, we all signaled along with her, everybody turning right one person at a time. My hand was the only bandaged one that didn't fit into the group. This time we were riding along a road that had much less traffic so we were able to ride more in pairs and groups.

The sun was getting hotter and even though there was a nice breeze, I could feel that my hair was full of sweat under my helmet. If this plan worked, I hoped no one was there to get my picture for the paper because I'm sure I would look atrocious.

After a few bursts of energy that left me mostly breathless, I ended up riding next to Susie. She had a smile on her face, but she seemed tense. Her hands were clutching her handlebars so tightly that her knuckles were white.

"Hi Tessa," she said. "I would ask about your hands but there is no time for conversation. I need to keep our pace."

"Oh that's alright," I said, trying not to huff and puff. "I'll just ride along with you. It's been nice getting back on a bike. Thanks for lending one to me. And my hands are okay, just a little accident."

Susie nodded, looking straight ahead. Even though our pace wasn't that fast, Susie was not interested in making conversation. That was fine with me. I had one thing that I needed to make sure of before we got to our destination. It was the final piece of the puzzle, just to make sure my hunch was right before we put the plan into place.

Unfortunately, I couldn't confirm it until we stopped or at least slowed down a little bit. I might have remembered how to ride a bicycle and I might even be having a little fun doing it, but I couldn't do more than one thing at a time.

We went up and down a few rolling hills. Sweat was pouring down the back of the red polo shirt I had borrowed from Sally. I hoped it wasn't a new shirt or else I would have rivers of red dye down my back. That was probably preferable to the red sunburn I had figured I would bring home from vacation, although I hadn't had any time to sunbathe.

My thoughts turned to sun burn as I focused on how hot my face felt. I hadn't put any sunscreen on before the bike ride, which was proving to be a mistake. We had been riding into the sun the entire time. I just hoped my face wouldn't be peeling when Max picked me up at home. Shedding my face skin may be the ultimate test to make sure he is worthy to marry, I suppose. If he could love me through that, he could love me through anything.

Susie stuck her arm out and made the stop signal. I put my bandaged hand out to signal a stop also. Up ahead, there was a four-way intersection with stop signs on each side. We slowed to a stop and I took the chance to check for the last clue I needed.

Once my bike was at a complete stop next to Susie, I looked over at her neck. Bouncing over her red shirt on her chest was a necklace with a bike charm dangling from it, matching the one I had seen on the security tape. Gotcha.

•Chapter Thirty-Three•

The rest of the bike ride was a bit of a blur. Once I saw the necklace that Susie was wearing and confirmed that it matched the necklace I saw on the person in the security tape, I had to wait until we reached our destination before I could make the rest of the plan work.

I stayed next to Susie for the rest of the ride, worried that if I backed off she would either get suspicious of me or that I would somehow lose her. The beginning of the ride had been pretty easy but the further we rode, the more winded I got. It was a good kind of tired though, and I was still seriously considering buying a bike to get me around Shady Lake next summer.

As we rode on, I tried to focus and think about why Susie would have been at the pool after Louise. Had she been the one to actually kill Hilda? Why had she been wet after she left the pool that night? There were so many questions. I just hoped that the questions would be answered soon.

After what seemed like an eternity of bike riding, we turned onto a road that had a big sign next to it announcing that we had made it to our destination. The picnic was going to be at a state park a bit out of the city. The Bike Brigade had rented a picnic shelter there for a few hours so that everyone could sit in the shade while we prepared to ride back all the way back to the park. My poor sunburnt nose would thank them for the shade.

There were a few cars parked outside next to the picnic shelter, mostly the club members who had volunteered to drive over the food and other provisions for the picnic. But there was one car with tinted windows that just had to be Officer Mendoza. I flashed as much of a thumbs-up as I could make towards the car so he would know I had visual confirmation of the necklace. I couldn't see inside the car, so I wondered if Officer Johnson was along. He may be pretty vanilla, but that didn't mean he was a bad cop. I really should cut him a little slack, but I had been worried that he wouldn't want to go along with our plan.

I pulled my bike around the the side of the picnic shelter and parked it with all of the other bikes. Even though I had come up with the basics of the plan, Officer Mendoza was the one who would make sure it all worked which included timing things just right. I was depending on him to make it all come together.

A few of the permanent grills around the picnic shelter were already full of meat with some of the men of the club tending them. Hamburgers, hot dogs, and bratwursts all had their own grills and the barbecuers dutifully turned and poked and prodded them until they were deemed done and put on platters, ready to be eaten.

As lunch was cooking and being set up, I wandered around making small talk and trying not to be nervous. Susie was also milling around the crowd and I wasn't sure if it was just me, but she seemed to be giving me a wide berth. Or I may have just been hyper aware of her whereabouts. Either way, I kept my eye on Susie.

Even though I had eaten a bigger breakfast to fuel up for the ride, I was famished after all of that. I loaded up my plate with potato chips, a hamburger, and a bar for dessert. Lunch was delicious even though I could barely taste it because I ate it so fast. I did take the time to savor my dessert, which was the kind of bar that had cereal and peanut butter as a base layer with a nice, thick, chocolate frosting. My fingers were covered with thick chocolate after eating one of those in the Florida heat. As much as I would have loved to lick all of the chocolate off of my fingers, I resisted the temptation and used a napkin to wipe them off instead.

Now I was starting to get antsy. When would Officer Mendoza put our plan into place? It felt like it was taking forever and the longer it took, the more nervous I got. The officers would need to show themselves soon.

"Hello there," Susie's voice suddenly boomed around the picnic shelter. Apparently there was a speaker system in place. "I'd just like to welcome everyone to the end of the year picnic for the Bike Brigade."

A light amount of applause came from the audience as I looked around, finally spotting Susie standing next to the table of desserts holding a microphone. She still looked nervous like she had before but for all I knew it was unrelated to our plan and she just had a fear of public speaking.

"Before we get to the raffle and some of the games, I'd just like to talk a little bit about this year's Bike Brigade and some of the fun things we all did together," Susie said, running her fingers through her sweaty hair.

She pulled out a piece of paper and started reading off trips they had taken together. Honestly, it sounded pretty fun and I thought that if there wasn't already a bike club in Shady Lake, I should start one after I buy my bicycle. I was scanning the crowd when I noticed that someone in the car with tinted windows was trying to get my attention. Susie was busy with her spiel, so I took the chance to sneak out of the shelter and over to the car.

The front window rolled down just enough so I could see Officer Mendoza in the driver's seat. Next to him was a grumpy looking Officer Johnson while

Louise was waving frantically at me from the backseat. Well, the gang was all here.

"Tessa, I saw what looked like a thumbs up and I am assuming that means you saw the necklace?" Officer Mendoza asked. Normally, he was in a happy, smiley mood but today he was all business. His face was set in a serious, eyebrow furrowing expression. There would be no joking around before the plan went down.

"Yes, it was definitely her necklace I saw on the security tape," I said. "I'm not sure what she did, but she was definitely in the pool area on the night of Hilda's murder."

"Louise, are you ready to do your part?" Officer Mendoza asked.

I bent down a little to see Louise a bit better. She was chewing her lip, but nodded her head.

"I'm ready," Louise said. "Justice needs to be done, for Hilda."

"Let's just hope this works," Officer Johnson said. "This plan isn't that much of a plan and I'm still not sure why we are depending so much on this civilian with the broken hands."

Officer Johnson sat scowling at me from the front seat. He alternated between giving me the stink eye and pretending I wasn't there. To be honest, I understood why he was so skeptical. In Shady Lake, the police officers knew me and knew they could trust me if it came to that. But down here in Florida, they didn't know me from Sam. I was some lady who waltzed into a murder investigation to help. And the plan I came up with wasn't really a plan, it was more of a very basic idea of a plan that we were mostly going to wing.

But I did have one thing going for me: for some reason Officer Mendoza believed in me. I'm not exactly sure why other than maybe he was like me and he followed his gut instinct. Either way, Susie wasn't going to stand up there and speak forever. We needed to get this plan rolling or it might not work at all.

•Chapter Thirty-Four•

I took a deep breath and prepared for my part of the plan. Everyone was still munching on their lunches, listening to Susie. I hadn't really been listening to what she was saying, but at this point she had to be wrapping up. It was now or never if we wanted this to work.

Winding my way through the picnic tables, I made my way to the front of the crowd. When Susie spotted me, she suddenly stopped talking and looked at me like I was some sort of idiot. I kind of felt like an idiot, but this was all part of the plan.

I reached out with both hands and grabbed the microphone out of Susie's hand. She was so surprised she didn't even try to stop me so I took the opportunity to wrap one arm around her shoulders so that she couldn't walk away when she realized what was about to happen. I struggled to hold the microphone in just one hand since it was still bandaged, but I needed to make sure that Susie stayed next to me.

"I'm so sorry to interrupt, but I have a few things to say," I said. I tried to make my voice so syrupy sweet that it almost dripped, hoping the crowd would go along with me. "First of all, my name is Tessa and I am staying with Bill and Sally. I'm best friends with their daughter Mandy. Second of all, let's just give a round of applause for Susie and everything she does for this club."

The crowd went along with me and applauded for Susie, who waved one hand in confusion. There were even a few cheers from some of the more enthusiastic Bike Brigade members. I waited for the noise to die down before I continued on. This was the key part of the plan. Taking a big breath, I continued on.

"Now, I have a surprise for everyone," I said. I plastered a big smile on my face. "We have a special guest here today that most of you probably already know. I'm pleased to announce that Louise Templeton is here, fresh from the police station."

Louise took her cue beautifully, emerging from behind the picnic shelter wall and walking slowly through the crowd. She waved like a star to her adoring fans as she slowly floated through the crowd. I was pleased to see she was met with smiles and waves from most of the people she passed by. Louise's biggest desire in life was to be loved and accepted and she deserved that.

I glanced at Susie to see that her face registered absolute shock. Her mouth was open and she looked dumbfounded. I could see that she was trying to figure out what was going on. A few obscenities came out under her breath as I could see that she was trying to figure out why Louise had been let out and whether anyone knew about her connection to the murder.

Louise finally got to the front of the crowd and stood on the other side of Susie, hemming her in so that she was stuck between the two of us. I could feel Susie tense up. She was so nervous that it was almost like she was a caged wild animal.

"If anyone didn't know, Louise was being held as a suspect in Hilda's murder," I said. I tried to sound as upbeat as possible so I didn't spoil the picnic mood, but it was hard to be positive about someone being murdered. "But now she has been released because new evidence has come to light."

"I will tell my side of the story because I know everyone is curious," Louise said. She was lapping up the spotlight. I supposed it was her moment to shine, in a completely weird way. "I saw Hilda in the pool area and I went in to give her a piece of my mind. It got a little heated and I'm ashamed to admit that I shoved her. She fell over and hit her head but that was when I left. I got scared and I ran home, bumping into Susie on the way who was kind enough to escort me the rest of the way."

Louise turned to look at Susie, her eyes filled with warmth. She reached out and put her hand on Susie's shoulder. Susie was trying to avoid looking at Louise and when she felt Louise's touch, she flinched

241

away. I was holding her tight enough that she couldn't move far. Instead, Susie dropped her gaze to the ground. I hoped that our plan would start working soon because I didn't want this to become too much of a public spectacle.

"It took a little while for this all to get straightened out with the police," Louise said with an odd laugh. "Obviously it looked like I was the one who had murdered Hilda. I'll be the first to admit that I should not have pushed her, but when I left she was alive and well. That means that someone out there was the one who killed Hilda and instead of doing the right thing and turning themselves in, they are letting people like me and Mandy take the fall for it."

Susie shifted nervously from foot to foot and I tried to keep a hold on her shoulder through my bandages. We were getting to the end of the plan, so all I could do was hope it was working it's magic on Susie. The plan had simply been to guilt Susie about the murder without actually telling her we knew she did it. If all went right, she would be willing to talk after this.

"If we could all take a moment of silence to remember Hilda, I think that would be nice," Louise said.

She lowered the microphone down and shut her eyes. The entire picnic pavilion went silent and I watched as most of the crowd closed their eyes along with Louise. Instead of going along with it, I leaned over and whispered in Susie's ear.

"There are two men here who would like to talk to you," I said. "I'll walk you over there once this moment of silence is over."

Susie glanced over at me with tears in her eyes and nodded. She seemed lighter, like a weight had been lifted off of her shoulders. I wasn't sure what exactly had happened between Susie and Hilda, but I knew that carrying around the secret must have been torture.

"Thank you," Louise said. "And now if someone could come take over the microphone for the raffle and games, I would surely appreciate it."

Laughter ran through the crowd as Louise smiled a rakish smile. This was her moment in the spotlight, cleared of being a murder suspect and she did not want to give it up. I threw a wink her way and escorted Susie out of the picnic shelter and into the capable hands of Officer Mendoza.

Officer Johnson read Susie her rights as they brought her to the car and had her climb into the backseat. As he closed the door, she lowered her head and cried. In that moment, I think we were all relieved that the truth was about to come out. The muffled shouts behind us meant that the games had started, but it was dimmed by the sight of Susie. Louise appeared next to me and slipped her arm through mine.

"Thank you, Tessa," she said. "The police officers told me that you were the reason I was let out. You were the one who figured out the truth. Also, I'd just like to say that I'm sorry about your hands."

"I'm still not exactly sure what the truth is," I admitted. "But I'm just glad that you and Mandy were both proven to be innocent. When terrible things like Hilda's death happen, the real killer should be held accountable. And no worries about my hands. The bandages look worse than my hands actually are."

The hot afternoon sun beat down, actually feeling good for once. I had sweat completely through my polo shirt during the bike ride and once I sat in the shade, it had all become cold against my skin. Sally might never be able to get this shirt completely clean so it might just have to come back to Shady Lake with me.

Louise and I stood with arms intertwined as Officer Mendoza backed out of the parking spot and slowly drove out of the park. I gave a little wave and was surprised to get one curt wave back from Officer Johnson. In the backseat, we could only see the back of Susie's head as she hid her face in her hands. My heart broke a little bit, but in some way she had done the crime and now she would have to do the time.

"I suppose the only way for me to get back to the park is for me to ride Susie's bike, isn't it?" Louise asked.

We had a bittersweet laugh together as we watched the car with Hilda's killer roll out of the park. I only had two days left of my vacation, but I could finally relax.

•Chapter Thirty-Five•

The morning after the Bike Brigade picnic, I was finally able to sleep in. There was nothing to be nervous about and I didn't have anything like a murder to mull over and lose sleep. When I woke up, the sun was already up and while I hadn't slept the day away, I could officially say I slept in.

I was the last one out on the deck that morning after I go dressed and changed the bandages on my hands. Bill, Sally, Mandy, and even Trevor were all soaking in the morning sun with cups of coffee. Despite the "only four chairs on the deck" rule, we pulled another out so that we could all sit together outside.

"I've got some things inside for us to munch on for brunch," Sally said once I was cozied into my chair. "Why don't I run inside and bring the food out? We were just waiting for you to get out of bed."

"I'll help you," Trevor said, jumping out of his chair to hold the door open for Sally.

Mandy smiled dreamily after him, playing with her engagement ring. She twirled it around her finger as she seemed to be daydreaming. I couldn't help but smile too. Now that the investigation was over, we could finally start to focus on the wedding.

I closed my eyes and basked in the sun while I

thought about when Peter and I had gotten engaged. We had been dating for a few years and we had both just graduated college, ready to start our first adult jobs. Peter took me to a special dinner where we got a private table overlooking the city. He did the classic "ring in a glass of champagne" proposal and even though I'd seen that in a bunch of movies, I loved it. It was classy and fun and I felt so mature even though we were still just kids.

Tears started to build up under my eyelids which I squeezed shut even tighter, hoping to keep the tears in. It did the opposite, making the tears run down my cheeks. I felt them slowly trickle down as I remembered the excitement, the butterflies in my stomach for weeks, the absolute puppy love.

Peter's face came into my mind and I sucked in a deep breath. He was so handsome. I missed him so much. Waves of sadness started to wash over me, sucking me down. I would have wallowed in it for a while until I felt a hand on my shoulder.

The physical touch pulled me out of the muck and when I opened my eyes, Mandy was sitting next to me with her hand on my shoulder. Her eyes were concerned, searching my face to figure out what was going on. I wiped away the tears on my cheeks with a sniffle.

"Are you alright?" she asked.

"I was just remembering Peter," I said. "I was

thinking about when we got engaged."

Mandy nodded. She had been the first one I called after we were engaged. I had been sniffling and sobbing into the phone and she had started crying too. For months after that, Mandy and I had spent hours upon hours on the phone together, planning my wedding. Now here we were with our roles reversed.

The door to the sunroom opened and Sally came out with a big metal tray loaded down with food. There were bowls of scrambled eggs and bacon, plates of cinnamon rolls and buttered toast. Trevor was close behind with a carafe of coffee and a big smile on his face. If I had a camera in that moment, I would have taken a picture of them coming out the door.

Instead, I took a mental picture so that I could remember the end of this crazy vacation. I also wanted to remember Trevor in this helpful way instead of his lazy way. Even though this week had turned out completely different from the relaxing getaway it was supposed to be, one thing it did was to help me see Trevor in a better light. I smiled at him as he topped up my cup of coffee.

"Don't look now, but we have a few more guests coming," Sally said. She waved toward the road with a smile.

Of course, the first thing we all did was look

down the road and try to figure out who Sally was talking about. There was the car with the tinted windows from the day before with Officer Johnson and Officer Mendoza inside.

But the most shocking person headed this way was Cindy on her new red bike. She was scowling towards us as she rode in front of the car of police officers. Between the frown on her face and the blank face on Officer Johnson's face, it was like a parade of grumpy people. How Officer Mendoza got roped into it, I would never know because he was riding in the car with a big, wide smile on his face.

The strange parade pulled up to the RV and Officer Mendoza hung out the passenger window. He looked so excited, almost like a big, happy dog who had been taken for a ride. It was nice to see him back as his happy-go-lucky self instead of the business self he had been yesterday.

"Hello there," he shouted. "I hope you don't mind if we join you. We may have also invited Cindy along"

"No problem, come on up," Sally said. "There's enough food for everyone."

The strange crew headed up the stairs. Bill and Trevor jumped up to grab extra chairs out of the sunroom so that everyone could join us for brunch. Cindy's face puckered up as I could see her silently counting the chairs on the deck. I knew she just wanted to be able to write it down for her next infraction report.

"I hope it's alright if we all sit together," Sally said, also realizing what Cindy was doing. "We would love to have you and the Officers join us."

Cindy harrumphed out a sigh before she plopped down in the chair Bill brought out for her. Mandy ran inside to grab a few more plates while I sat with my bandaged hands, feeling rather useless. Within minutes, we were all happily munching on our food. I'm not sure when Sally had made all of this, but apparently I had slept through it.

"So, we do have an actual reason why we came," Officer Mendoza said. "And it wasn't just to eat all of your food. We came to let you know what actually happened to Hilda."

The table went quiet; even Trevor stopped eating for a moment. We all looked up at Officer Mendoza, giving him our full attention. I had kind of assumed I would have to go back to Minnesota without really knowing what had happened. Officer Mendoza launched into the story that Susie had told him about Hilda's murder.

*****

After Susie had found a distraught Louise the night of the dance and helped her home, she noticed that Louise was missing her special pin. Once Roger arrived home to help Louise, Susie figured she would go back out to look for it in the last place she had seen Louise come out of; the pool area.

When she went through the pool gate, she spotted Louise's pin under a chair but she was surprised to find Hilda sitting in a deck chair holding her head. Hilda told her what Louise had done and started threatening Louise. Susie jumped to Louise's defense and when Hilda got up and into her face, Susie decided she needed to leave the pool area.

But when she turned to leave, Hilda grabbed her by the arm. They started to struggle and in the struggle they both ended up falling into the pool. Susie is athletic and a strong swimmer, but apparently Hilda couldn't swim and she started to panic. The scratches and other signs of a struggle on Hilda weren't from a fight with Susie, but from her fight for survival.

Susie knew that if she didn't get away, they would both drown, so she managed to untangle herself from Hilda and swim to the shallow end. She climbed out as fast as she could and raced around the edge of the pool to help Hilda get out.

The closest thing she could grab was Mandy's pool noodle, which happened to be on the ground next to the pool. Susie extended it out, but Hilda was already so weak from trying to tread water and from the bump she had received on her head that she couldn't manage to grab onto it. Susie said that

251

eventually Hilda must have given up because all of a sudden, she was very still.

At that point, Susie panicked. Instead of getting help and explaining what had happened, she left and snuck her way home so she didn't run into anyone. She said it was almost like an out of body experience; that something was propelling her home instead of finding someone to help her.

Susie sat up all night trying to figure out what she should do but before she could think of a plan, she heard Sally's scream and ran to join everyone at the pool. At that point, Susie was caught in a web of lies that unfolded out of her control. She didn't want anyone else to be arrested for what happened but she also knew that she had not handled the situation well and that she would be in trouble if she came forward at that point.

So Susie lived in a panic for days, simultaneously trying to cover things up and also help get Mandy and Louise released from custody. Every time she tried to make things better, it just got more complicated. At the picnic, she was ready for it all to be over. So when Louise showed up that afternoon, Susie was relieved for the entire thing to come to an end.

*****

We all sat on the deck, none of us having touched our food as Officer Mendoza told the story.

What a horrible situation to have to witness play out. I couldn't imagine watching someone drown. And while Susie made the absolute wrong decision that night, some people naturally panic in emergency situations. I was glad to know that she hadn't murdered Hilda, but I was also upset that she had almost tried to cover it all up, unknowingly throwing innocent people under the bus along the way.

"So it was all an accident," Cindy said. "I had no idea she didn't know how to swim."

She had been so quiet that I had almost forgotten she was there. I was used to her loud, in-your-face brashness but in grief, her personality was a bit more subdued.

"I don't think anyone knew," Sally said, patting Cindy's hand in sympathy. "But that would explain why she hated the pool and bobbing so much."

We all slowly went back to eating brunch, although the mood was a bit heavier now. Hilda's death hung over all of us, a reminder that life can come to an end so suddenly. The feeling was dark in contrast to the bright, warm morning.

"I'd like to say something if I could," Officer Johnson said, folding his hands in front of him on the table.

Officer Mendoza gave him an odd look that mirrored what the rest of us were thinking. I got the feeling that Officer Johnson wasn't much of a talker, so whatever he wanted to say must be important.

"Tessa, I just wanted to say that you did a pretty okay job on this," he said, which sounded like high praise coming from him. "I'm not a verbose man, so I'll just say it one time; thank you."

I smiled, feeling my cheeks redden. Bill, Sally, Mandy, and even Cindy clapped a little bit while Trevor started in on a rollicking rendition of "For She's a Jolly Good Fellow." Once he finished singing, Officer Mendoza put his fingers between his lips and whistled, the sound cracking the mid-morning air.

We all laughed and for once, I felt like my busybody ways were actually cheered on by a few people. That might not be such a good thing, considering I have an even longer list of people who wished I would not look into these crimes quite as close. Despite my mother's support on this one, she was at the top of the list of people who hated when I investigated.

•Chapter Thirty-Six•

The sun was setting on Shady Lake and while it was a warm spring day, it was nothing compared to the warmth I had left behind in Florida. One thing Minnesota did have was the handsome man sitting next to me. Max and I were sitting in the front window of the B&B, holding hands and watching the sun set over the lake. Well, I guess I should say that Max was holding my bandage because my hands were still pretty sore and wrapped up.

We had already gone out for an early dinner because ever since I got home early in the morning, we had spent the entire day together. It felt comfortable and perfect even though my hands were mostly useless.

I had even told Max the entire story about my meddling down in Florida and while he tsk-tsked me and my nosiness, he couldn't help but laugh at my inability to even take a vacation. He also thought the story of my tea catching incident were pretty funny, even though he wished he could hold my hand without the bandages. I laughed along with him, just happy to be with him. Now here we were at the end of our day together.

"I think I'm going to buy a bike this summer," I said. "I kind of enjoyed riding one down in Florida."

"As long as you wear a helmet, Officer Max will approve that," he said, pretending to be stern.

"Jokes on you, I'm buying a bicycle built for two," I said.

"I'm sure Mandy will love riding that around town with you," Max said with a mischievous smile on his face.

I threw my head back and laughed. Max was so quick with a comeback sometimes that it caught me totally off-guard. When I managed to look at him, he was intently watching me laugh. Max's blue eyes were soft and his face had a smile so wide it was about to burst. It was a look of absolute love.

"I have a feeling that Mandy and I will be doing more wedding planning than anything this summer," I said. "She and Trevor want to get married by the end of summer. They figure they've been together long enough that they don't want to wait too long to make it official."

"I can understand that," Max said, squeezing my hand just gently enough so that I could feel it through my bandages. "We've been waiting a long time too."

The butterflies in my stomach were back, trying to pound their way out along with my heart. This was the first time we had talked about our future together in person. Over the phone, it was so easy to say whatever without seeing the other person. But face to face it was different, almost like it was too real.

"I want to marry you someday Tessa," Max said. He pulled me out of my chair and over to his lap. I nestled into him. "I hope it's alright if that someday might be sooner rather than later."

"I guess that would be alright," I said, tilting my face up to kiss him. "As long as you know what you're in for, we should be able to make that happen."

A cough from behind us made us jump. Startled I turned around to find my father's back facing us.

"Hello lovebirds," he said. "Sorry to interrupt, but I'd like to invite you to join us for dessert and games in the living room. Fun will be had by all. I know that because I have made it mandatory."

I giggled and stood up, grabbing Max's hand and pulled him up out of the chair with me.

"It's alright Dad, it's safe to turn around," I said, knowing that he was trying very hard to not see his little girl wrapped up in the arms of her lover.

He turned around with a big, cheesy grin on his face. I knew it was partially because he was so happy to see me back with Max. Peter had been great and Clark had been alright, but Max had been around the family so long that he was a part of the family even when he had been married to someone else.

The three of us walked into the living room where my mom and a few of the guests of the bed and breakfast were eating sweets and deciding on what games to play. The living room was homey and welcoming with comfy pillows and warm blankets strewn about for anyone to make a nest out of. A fire was crackling in the fireplace and outside the window a few snow flurries were falling. While snow may not sound great in spring, I have a personal rule that snow is always magical no matter what month it falls in.

I looked around the room. Florida had been a fun change of pace. The warm weather and getting to be outside and in the pool were such a change from the cold spring in Minnesota. But I was glad to be back. Even though there were a few strangers among us, this was home.

•About the Author•

Linnea West lives in Minnesota with her husband and two children. She taught herself to read at the age of four and published her first poem in a local newspaper at the age of seven. After a turn as a writer for her high school newspaper, she went to school for English Education and Elementary Education. She didn't start writing fiction until she was a full time working mother. Besides reading and writing, she spends her time chasing after her children, watching movies with her husband, and doing puzzle books. Learn more about her and her upcoming books by visiting her website and signing up for her newsletter at linneawestbooks.com.

Note From the Author: Reviews are gold to authors! If you've enjoyed this book, would you consider rating it and reviewing it on Amazon? Thank you!

•Other Books in the Series•

Small Town Minnesota Cozy Mystery Series
Book One-Halloween Hayride Murder
Book Two-Christmas Shop Murder
Book Three-Winter Festival Murder
Book Four-Valentine's Blizzard Murder
Book Five-Spring Break Murder